Lambs Fighting Wolves

Debbie Beeber

ISBN 978-1-64416-182-1 (paperback)
ISBN 978-1-64416-183-8 (digital)

Christian Faith Publishing, Inc.
832 Park Avenue
Meadville, PA 16335
www.christianfaithpublishing.com

Printed in the United States of America

Chapter 1

Kaylee tucked the afghan around her grandmother's legs and kissed her cheek. "OK, Grammie, I'll be back later."

"Where are you off to? It's already 9 p.m."

Kaylee sighed. She adored her grandmother, but her memory lapses were starting to get annoying. Actually, when she let herself think about it, annoying was not the word. She was terrified. What would happen to Grammie if her grandmother had Alzheimer's? What would happen to Kaylee if her grandmother had to be in assisted living? She was only sixteen. Live in foster care for two years? How could she live through another loss? She shook her head to derail her train of thought. "Remember I told you that everyone is going to a party?"

Grammie turned her head as if listening to someone to her right. She subtly nodded in agreement and then focused on Kaylee. "I don't think that is a good idea. There will be drinking, and nothing good will come of it. They will take you away from me if you keep getting into trouble."

Kaylee clinched her teeth. "Skipping class a couple of times is not a big deal, Grammie."

Grammie smiled. "Sweetheart, I just want you to be the best you can be."

Kaylee smiled back. "I know. Thanks, Grammie." She bent down and kissed the soft, wrinkled cheek, smelling the rose perfumed powder. She stood and creased her forehead. "You going to be OK by yourself?"

Grammie smiled. "I'm never alone, sweetheart." She glanced to her right. "I always have my Guardian Angel."

Kaylee sighed. "Yeah, well, if he gets you some tea later, remind him to turn off the burner."

The TV news anchor caught Grammie's attention. "The government has just announced the expansion of an initiative to address the foreclosure epidemic and clean up our neighborhoods. Citizens had complained that abandoned houses were a magnet for crime, so the government tore down those homes and put up affordable single person apartments. They feature a fantastic new idea of common areas for recreation and eating and single rooms for sleeping. It's much like dormitory living that has been so successful in China. Detroit was the first city to implement this program after its collapse. California, Chicago, and New York were not far behind and have functioning structures in the heart of the cities. The government has decreed this program a success and will expand to the suburbs and small towns, announcing today that these life-saving buildings will be in every locality, fundamentally transforming America's neighborhoods. We can all agree that this is a wonderful new program."

"That's all we need," Grammie clucked her tongue in disgust, putting down her knitting for the new prayer shawl she was working on for her ladies' club at church. "'Successful like China'… never thought I'd live to see America trying to be like China. And single-person apartments… what about families? Why aren't they important anymore? Why don't they report how families are split up in those places? Now they're starting to build one of those atrocious things across the street. It's like they are trying to make us all be alone." Grammie glanced to her right and nodded. She grasped Kaylee's hand. "You are never alone, Sweetheart. Just ask and your Guardian Angel will help."

Kaylee shook her head and smiled. She wanted to leave before Grammie went on one of her "America is changing" rants. She crossed the small family room and went out of the garage door, the two steps creaking loudly as she descended because there was no one to fix them.

You should stay home and avoid temptation.

Kaylee dug in her purse for her car keys. "Where are those stupid keys?!"

Exasperated, she went into the house and looked under every pile of paper and in every drawer in the kitchen. Hands on her hips, she stood in the middle of the room. Finally, she took her purse and dumped it on the table.

"There you are!" She grabbed the items on the table and shoved them back in her purse, irritated. She slammed the car door. The engine made a grinding noise but wouldn't turn over. She tried again. She dropped her head in disbelief.

"Come on, Guardian Angel," she mocked. "Kaylee needs to have a good time tonight."

After the fifth time, she slammed the steering wheel in defeat. She pulled out her phone and texted her best friend, Mandy. *Hey, stupid car won't start. Can you pick me up?*

There was a pause and then she read *Nope, sorry, got a ride and already here. Let me see if I can get someone's keys.*

Kaylee smiled and texted *Thx.* She got out of the car and went to sit on the porch swing to wait. The cicadas started their strange chorus, building louder and louder, went silent, then started again. She wrinkled her nose. "Creepy things."

Kaylee looked down her sleepy street. It was so different now. Foreclosure signs were waving in most of the yards; some of them abandoned and unkept, others filled with terrified families waiting for the bank to throw them out onto the street. She gazed at the large foundation for the new government housing structure across the street, gobbling up the family homes that were once enjoying the space. It was cold and heartless compared to her tiny home. She shivered.

"I wonder if Grammie is right." She imagined what the neighborhood would look like with no single-family homes and people living in big dormitories like in China. She smiled. "Maybe we'd finally get some decent Chinese restaurants."

A car door slammed a few houses away, catching her attention. The engine roared, and a rap song blared. Kaylee smiled, leaped from the swinging bench, and ran to the curb. The car screeched to a stop in front of her.

"Hey," A dark-haired teen casually leaned an arm out of the window as he blew smoke in her direction.

"You passed your driver's test!"

"Fourth time is a charm," he smiled. "Going to Urlacher's party?"

"Trying, but my car won't start."

"Hop in."

Kaylee ran to the other side and jumped in. "Thanks!"

"No problem," he shouted over the music as he stepped on the gas.

This is not a good idea. He drives way too fast, and later, he will most likely be drunk!

Kaylee gently shook her head to rid herself of the thought. She texted *Gr8 news. Darius picked me up and wr on r way!* A moment later, her phone chimed, and she smiled at the *Oooo he's hot* ☺.

As they got closer to the party, the houses morphed into two-story four-car garaged confirmations that the only Americans who were avoiding foreclosures worked in big business with government connections. No plumbers, teachers, or small business people lived in this Camelot, and they were certainly not welcomed at the round table. Kaylee lurched forward as Darius slammed on the brakes to park. She slowly got out of the car and self-consciously smoothed out her shirt. Her entire house could fit into the living room here. The house was alive with light and sound; teens were everywhere. She texted *where r u.*

"See you," Darius nodded her way as he grabbed a red Solo cup of beer from a small group of guys that greeted him warmly.

Kaylee glanced up and smiled, "Yeah, thanks again, Darius."

Kaylee's phone chimed and she looked down, *By the pool.* She turned sideways to squeeze through the crowd. As she made her way to the crowded pool area, she heard the group chant "drink, drink, drink, drink!" and cheered as Mandy triumphantly held up the empty pitcher to hoots and yells. She saw Kaylee and screamed in delight as she hugged her. "My best friend! Everyone, my best friend is here!" She grabbed a full pitcher and pushed it into Kaylee's hands. "You're next! You're next!" The crowd cheered. Kaylee laughed and held up the pitcher before she started to chug. The crowd cheered and chanted "drink, drink, drink, drink!" until she gulped the last of the beer and held the pitcher high above her head to the applause.

Mandy tried to high five her, missed, laughed, and fell into her arms. "How wasted am I?" she laughed.

Kaylee fist punched the air, "Whoop-whoop!"

Enough, we should go.

Kaylee laughed at the thought as she grabbed a shot from the table. "No way. I'm going to have a good time."

"What?" slurred Mandy.

Kaylee leaned closer and yelled above the music, "I said we are going to have a good time!"

"Hell, yeah, we are!"

An hour later, Kaylee was listening to Darius tell a funny story about how Mrs. Whitman was on his case for not doing his social studies homework. "So she says to me, 'Mr. King, how will you know if your rights are being violated if you don't know them?' And I said to her, 'The only right I care about is my right to party!'"

As the crowd cheered, Darius punched up his hand, which was holding his beer and more than half of it splashed onto him and Kaylee. The crowd laughed and cheered again.

Darius leaned in towards Kaylee, "Hey, I'm sorry!"

Kaylee giggled and slurred, "No problem."

"Let's go upstairs and see if we can score some dry shirts."

They stumbled and maneuvered through the teens until they made it upstairs to a bedroom. They laughed as they fell into the room. Kaylee glanced at the posters of sports cars with girls in bikinis sprawled across them and the trophies on the shelf, glowing with the faint light coming from a football nightlight.

"Must be Payton's room."

"No doubt," Darius said as he fumbled with the dresser drawer and rifled through the clothes. "OK, let's get you out of that wet shirt and into a dry one. Here's a Chicago Blackhawk's shirt for you. You a fan?" He turned towards her as she drunkenly took off her wet shirt.

Modesty! Whoa! Modesty!

"Of course I'm a fan! It's practically a requirement if you live here. Aren't you?" Kaylee watched as Darius's facial expression changed, dropping his good-hearted smile.

Modesty! Grab the shirt and quickly put it on. Get out of here!

Kaylee suddenly realized that Darius was staring at her bra and was self-conscious. "Umm, can I have that shirt?"

Darius closed the distance between them. She could smell the beer on his breath.

"I'm a fan of yours," his voice was husky as he leaned in to kiss her. Kaylee returned the kiss, her head feeling light and free. Darius was really cute and a star football player. Everyone loved him. Most girls would kill to be in her position right now.

Stop! Stop this right now!

Darius moved to her neck, sending electric shivers through her as he put one of his hands on her bottom and squeezed.

Whoa! Whoa! Modesty! Chastity!

Kaylee snapped to reality. "Whoa, whoa, Darius. I..."

Darius whispered in her ear, "Shhh, it's OK. It's OK."

This is not OK! Stop right now! You don't want to do this!

Kaylee gently pushed Darius back, "I'm sorry, but I don't think I want to do this."

Darius gently pulled her close. "Your kiss said you do."

Kaylee returned his kiss again, enjoying the feeling of losing herself in the moment. The door flew open and light filled the room. A couple giggled when they saw Kaylee with no shirt on.

"This room is taken!" Darius yelled.

Get out of here before you do something you can't take back.

"No, no, it isn't."

Darius tilted his head. "You sure?"

Kaylee nodded.

Darius gently touched her cheek. "Too bad." He held out the jersey.

She hastily pulled the shirt over her head. "Thanks, though, Darius. You're great, really. I just can't tonight. Thanks, though," as she awkwardly pulled away from him and past the eager couple who was still laughing.

Darius laughed and punched the guy playfully on the shoulder as he walked out of the room, "Hope you have better luck, dude."

Kaylee turned to a small group in the hall waiting to use the bathroom as Darius stumbled by and went down the stairs. She leaned against the wall and slowly slid down to sit, putting her hands over her face. She pictured her grandmother sitting in her recliner, the same recliner that Grammie read *Is your Mama a Llama* to Kaylee when she was young. She most likely was now reading her Bible and wondering what Kaylee was doing.

"What am I doing?" she mumbled. The past two years were so hard. First, her dad ran out on them, and they had to move in with Grammie. Then a few weeks later, her mom died in a car crash after working late on her news story. How can that happen in one family? She just wanted to forget and have fun for a night. Was that so bad? She needed to blow off some steam so she could handle her life. Grammie said God didn't give you more than you could handle.

"Well, I can't handle this anymore, God. Please help me." She chuckled. "I want my Guardian Angel to help me now." She leaned her head back against the wall and looked up to the ceiling. It was painted with a pretty design that almost looked like little white waves or clouds, a crystal chandelier sending sparkles around the professionally painted hallway. "Grammie deserves a house like this," she mumbled to herself.

"Long line for *el bano*?" A boy named Curtis plopped down next to Kaylee. "Hey, you look too serious. You losing your buzz? You need another drink."

Grammie wouldn't like this house. She likes her small house she shared with Grandpa.

Kaylee laughed, "You're right."

"Of course, I'm right," Curtis slurred.

Kaylee looked at Curtis as if she just realized he sat down. She caught her breath. The most handsome guy she ever saw was sitting between her and Curtis. Who was he? She would have definitely heard about him starting at school if he was a new student. Maybe he's Payton's cousin just visiting or something. He had light brownish hair that begged to have fingers run through it and the deepest blue green eyes.

"It's time to go," said the handsome guy, looking at her intently.

"Want me to get you a drink?" Curtis asked. A door opened, and a couple walked out of it, adjusting their shirts. "Or do you want to go in there?" He laughed.

"Go where?" Kaylee asked, looking at the handsome stranger.

Curtis laughed, "In there. Want to go in there with me?"

The stranger knitted his eyebrows and looked deeper into Kaylee's face. "Are you talking to me?"

Kaylee smiled at him, knowing that the buzz was making her much braver than she would be if she were completely sober. "Yes, you."

Curtis paused before he took a drink. He slowly put his drink down. "Really?"

"You can see me?" asked the stranger.

"Well, I'm buzzed but I'm not that buzzed," Kaylee giggled.

Curtis tilted his head. "So you don't?"

"Let's get out of here. We'll go for a walk to clear your head, just down the street to the park." The stranger smiled. Kaylee's heart skipped a beat. He was breathtaking.

"OK. Let's go," she said enthusiastically as she got up.

Curtis smiled. "Great!" And he hurried into the open room as Kaylee let the stranger guide her downstairs and out the front door.

The cool breeze hit her, and she breathed deeply. She smiled and waved to people as she left, trying to get as many of them to notice her with this handsome stranger as she could.

"That's better. You were getting into trouble in there," he smiled at her when they were away from the loud music.

Kaylee returned the smile, although knowing she couldn't match his. "My name is Kaylee."

The stranger looked at her and laughed as if what she said was absurd. "I know." Then he stopped suddenly and looked deeply into her eyes. "Do you really see me? You don't think you're alone right now?"

Kaylee stood on the sidewalk, not knowing what to say.

He kept staring into her eyes and started waving a hand in front of her face. "Do you see me? Do you hear me? Say my name. Say Cotravin."

Kaylee giggled. Even though this was sort of weird, he was so handsome that she found him charming.

"Oh," he put down his hand, disappointed. "For a minute there, I thought... I hoped..." He slowly began to walk, and Kaylee walked beside him. They walked for a couple of minutes in silence, but Kaylee noticed that it didn't seem awkward at all. She breathed deeply and paused as they came to the man-made lake at Harmony Park. She sat on the bench.

"I always liked it here," she whispered.

He followed her gaze and looked out onto the lake at a pair of ducks lazily swimming. "I know." He put one leg up on the bench and leaned on it.

"So what kind of name is Cotravin?"

He lost his balance in surprise. "What?!"

Kaylee looked at him and giggled. "Looks like I'm not the only one who's been drinking."

He peered into her eyes. "Say it again. Say my name."

"Cotravin. You know it's weird. It's a strange name, but it seems familiar somehow."

Cotravin let out a celebratory yell and punched at the sky like the teens during their drinking game. "Wow! Wow, I can't believe it! I've been waiting for so long!"

Kaylee enjoyed him. He was sweet, even though he was a bit confusing. "Waiting for what?"

"Waiting for you to talk to me again." He dropped to one knee and gazed tenderly into her eyes as if he just opened the best Christmas present in his life.

Kaylee raised her eyebrows. "Really?"

Cotravin slowly nodded his head, savoring the moment.

Kaylee tilted her head. "What do you mean for 'so long'?"

Cotravin whispered, "Since the beginning of time."

Kaylee breathed, "Wow."

Out of the corner of her eye, a man ran past her and grabbed the strap of her purse, jerking her sideways and almost pulling her off of the bench. He pulled at it, but it was around her neck and shoulder, and the strap would not break. He pulled out a knife and waved it in front of her. "Not too bright being here by yourself. Gimme that."

Kaylee caught her breath. Cotravin frowned and whistled. A big stray dog came out of the bush and growled. The man released the purse and slowly backed up, waving his knife. When he was at the edge of the line of bushes, he turned and disappeared around the corner.

Cotravin shook his head sadly and returned his gaze to Kaylee. "You OK?"

Kaylee nodded, shaking.

Cotravin smiled gently. "You should breathe now."

Kaylee sucked in a breath.

Cotravin looked at the big dog. "Thank you."

Kaylee was still shaking. "Is he... is he your dog?"

Cotravin tilted his head. "No. He just happens to live here around the lake. He's homeless. There are lots of homeless pets now. People just abandon them when they leave their foreclosed house."

Kaylee knitted her eyebrows in confusion. "I... how...?"

Cotravin looked at the dog as if they were having a conversation. "Hmm... that's a good idea." He looked at Kaylee. "Can he live with you and Grammie? He would make a great watchdog. And he did just save your life."

Kaylee looked between him and the dog. "What? How did you know about Grammie? I... can you take him?"

Cotravin looked at her and smiled. "You don't understand what I am yet, do you?"

"What are you?"

"I'm your Guardian Angel."

Kaylee laughed, "Actually, I think the dog there did most of the guarding."

Cotravin smiled. "But I asked him to."

Kaylee laughed again. "Oh, OK. You are the hero then."

Cotravin stood. "I'm your Guardian Angel."

Kaylee laughed again. "OK."

Cotravin looked at the dog and back to Kaylee. "Look at me."

Kaylee smiled.

Cotravin smiled and said softly, "No. Really look at me."

Kaylee looked at him. They were in a dimly lit area. She noticed his perfect white teeth, perfect hair, perfect eyes, his perfect white shirt... his perfect white pants. Huh. He likes white. He was incredibly handsome. And he shimmered with a sparkle like new fallen snow and... shimmered? She looked at him closer. She reached out to touch his hand, and her fingers touched nothing but air. She caught her breath.

"Are you a ghost?"

Cotravin chuckled, "No. I'm your Guardian Angel."

Kaylee waved her arm through him. The dog tilted his head and sat. Kaylee looked at the dog, "Do you see him?"

"Animals see angels."

"I don't believe in angels. This doesn't make sense."

"Oh, but believing I am a ghost was better?" Cotravin laughed. "And you have a big crush on that vampire character in that TV series you watch. You didn't question werewolves either," he folded his arms, "or walking zombies."

"That's different." Kaylee paused. "I think... I don't know."

"We should go. It's not safe here at night anymore." Cotravin glanced around.

"Are you saying there are vampires and werewolves?"

"No," Cotravin smirked. "I'm saying there are more criminals like the one who just tried to snatch your purse."

Kaylee slowly stood up and kept glancing at him as they walked back to the Urlacher house. Cotravin whistled, and the dog barked and ran up beside him. Kaylee casually kept putting her arm out to test if it went through him.

"Why do you keep doing that? I'm not solid."

"Then you're not real. Wow, I need to stop drinking."

"Well, yes, you should stop drinking. But I'm real. Air and gas aren't solid, and they're real."

13

"So you're gas?" Kaylee asked as they walked up the Urlacher's walkway.

"Sorry! You know how I get when I have too much beer," Mandy belched again. "All gas."

Kaylee directed her eyes to Mandy. "Do you see him?"

"Yes! He's so cute!" Mandy dropped to her knees, petting the dog as he licked her face. "Where'd you get him?"

"Not him," Kaylee nodded her head to her right, "Him."

Mandy looked up and knitted her eyebrows. "Who?"

"The perfect guy next to me."

Cotravin smirked, "Thank you."

"Uhh, either you are really drunk or I am," Mandy laughed as the dog covered her face with kisses. "There's just you, me, and this dog."

Kaylee rubbed her forehead, "I think I'm going to go home. I don't feel well. Have you seen Darius? I need to ask him if he'll drive me home."

"No! No, not him," Cotravin exclaimed.

"Well, how do you expect me to get home? Are you going to fly me home?" Kaylee put her hands on her hips and faced him.

Mandy watched in confusion.

"No, no. That's not allowed except on missions. I'll call someone who is sober." Cotravin put a hand up to his forehead, closed his eyes for a moment, and then opened them. "There. He'll be here in a minute."

"Do you get unlimited minutes calling people that way?" Kaylee mocked. "By the way, where are your wings?"

Mandy stopped petting the dog. "Hey, are you OK?"

Cotravin stood straight and flexed his shoulders. Wings spanning six feet popped out and spread from his shoulder blades. Kaylee jumped back, startled. Then curiosity overtook her, and she began to examine them.

"Wow, they look like the softest feathers. Are those feathers? I wish I could feel them. That is the purest white on top I've ever seen. How do you keep that so clean? And what color is that underneath?

Blues and greens like those pictures of the tropical sea. Beautiful... like your eyes." She came face to face with him and blushed.

"Kaylee, what are you talking about?" Mandy stood up.

Kaylee gestured with her thumb. "Him, he's my Guardian Angel... and he's gorgeous."

"Well, sure," Mandy laughed. "Why make him ugly?"

Kaylee laughed. "I think someone put something in the beer. This is not a normal buzz. I'm seeing things."

A burnt orange Cobalt pulled up to the curb, and the passenger window rolled down. The girls bent over to peer in.

"Hi, cowboy," Kaylee waved.

"Hey, Jordan!" Mandy slurred. "You finally coming to a party, deacon boy?"

Jordan smiled good-naturedly. "No. I came to pick up Kaylee."

Kaylee tilted her head, confused. "You did? How did you know I needed a ride?"

"Uhh... " Jordan stumbled, adjusting his cowboy hat. Even though he moved to Illinois from Texas a year ago, he couldn't give up his roots.

"I told you I called someone," Cotravin hastened, "Just get in."

Kaylee opened the door. The dog barked. "Oh, yeah. Can he come?"

"Sure."

Kaylee opened the back door, and the dog jumped in. She hugged Mandy goodbye and got in the passenger side. Jordan checked his side mirror and slowly pulled away. Kaylee rubbed her forehead.

"You OK?" Jordan glanced at her.

Kaylee stared at him. "How did you know I needed a ride?"

Jordan glanced at her nervously. "I just did."

She studied him, "Do you know Cotravin?"

"Who?"

"He doesn't know me," Cotravin said from the back seat.

Kaylee jumped, startling Jordan.

"What are you doing?" Jordan asked.

"Did you know that you have a Guardian Angel in your backseat?" She laughed.

"You can see him?" Jordan glanced sideways at her.

Kaylee stopped laughing. "You can see him?"

"He doesn't see me. He sees Fredouglass," Cotravin explained.

"Fredouglass?" Kaylee asked.

Jordan swerved then gained back control. "What did you say?"

"Fredouglass."

"You can hear Fredouglass?" Jordan asked, surprised.

"No. Who is Fredouglass?"

"He's who I called. He is Jordan's Guardian Angel," Cotravin explained.

"So you guys talk to each other?" Kaylee asked Cotravin.

"Yes," Jordan breathed, "this is incredible! I used to think I was crazy. But now you can hear Fredouglass, too. I was the only one who could hear him talk."

"No, not you," Kaylee let out her breath in frustration, "I can't talk to both of you at once!"

There was an uncomfortable silence.

"Well? Someone talk and explain this to me!" Kaylee demanded.

Jordan laughed, "I'm guessing you met your Guardian Angel tonight for the first time."

"You know about Guardian Angels?"

Jordan laughed again, "Uh, hello, I'm a deacon's kid. Sort of raised that way."

"Oh, yeah, right," Kaylee pondered. "Do you see Cotravin?"

"No. I only hear Fredouglass."

"So when did you meet Fredouglass?"

"I've always had him. I don't remember him not being by me."

Kaylee thought about this and glared at Cotravin. "Where have you been? I could have used you a few times, you know?" She wiped away a tear. "It's not easy having your dad take off on you and then your mom dying."

Cotravin was suddenly next to her even though there was no seat. "Beloved, I've always been with you. Remember me when you were little? But when you got a little older, you stopped believing. You just blocked seeing me until now. You still heard me, like earlier tonight."

Kaylee thought. "Oh, yeah. Mom said I had an imaginary friend… when I was little." She concentrated on her earliest memories; flashes of scenes went quickly through her mind. In one scene, she was about four years old, laughing and calling out Cotravin's name as they ran through a princess sprinkler. "That's why your name sounded familiar."

Cotravin nodded his head.

Kaylee looked ahead then back at him. "So… Grammie isn't losing her mind? She's talking to her Guardian Angel?"

Cotravin nodded.

"Anyone else know about this angel thing?"

Cotravin shrugged. "I know what I need to know to help you."

"You're not like all-seeing or all-powerful?"

Cotravin looked insulted, "I'm not God."

Kaylee thought. "Was that you with the keys earlier?"

Cotravin nodded.

"That was not funny!"

"I wasn't being funny," he explained. "I was trying to prevent you from going to the party."

Jordan cleared his throat, "Uh, sorry to interrupt, but you're home." Kaylee looked at him. He smiled. "I guess you're kinda freaked out right now."

She nodded her head.

"You never really had that since you always believed," Fredouglass explained.

Kaylee glanced back at him. He was also very good looking with dark skin and light brown eyes. He was also shimmering. "Wow. Are all of you so perfect?" she whispered.

"Who?" Jordan asked. "Can you see Fredouglass, too?"

Kaylee nodded.

"I've never seen him, just heard him."

"Odd," Fredouglass stated.

"Very," Cotravin added.

"You know what this means," Fredouglass looked concerned.

"Yes." Cotravin rubbed his chin in thought. "We better consult with Mikha'el tonight when our beloveds sleep."

"Who's Mikha'el?" asked Kaylee.

"Our general."

"You call him Michael," Fredouglass added.

"Michael?" Jordan's eyes widened. "You mean Michael the Archangel?"

"Yes." The angels answered.

"Holy sh—" The angels looked at Kaylee crossly. "I mean, wow, that's really… wow. Isn't Michael—"

"Mikha'el" the angels chorused.

"OK. Isn't Mikha'el the one who kicks Satan's a—… butt?" Kaylee asked.

"Yes. He is the lead general in the battle." Cotravin frowned. "Maybe you finally seeing me again isn't just coincidence tonight."

"That's what I'm thinking," Fredouglass agreed. "We might be in for something big."

Jordan's mouth opened in astonishment. "I… I see you now." He pointed to both angels.

The angels exchanged looks.

"The American Covenant must be in jeopardy," Fredouglass said.

Cotravin nodded, "This hasn't happened since Abraham."

"Abraham who?" Kaylee asked.

"Lincoln," the angels answered.

Kaylee and Jordan exchanged looks.

Chapter 2

The elderly man made a slight gesture of dismissal with his hand, making the servant hastily set down the silver tray holding an expensive tea set and scurry away from the mahogany desk. A hint of a smile crossed his wrinkled face. He enjoyed confirmation of his power, no matter how small. He returned his attention to the screen in front of him. Each section contained a head of state from all of the major countries.

"Mrs. Effluent," he interrupted, registering her flinch when he purposefully replaced the customary title of president with the informal. He never used their honorary titles; it reminded them that he gave them their positions, and he could easily take them away if they displeased him. "I grow weary of the delays."

The woman nervously cleared her throat and quickly patted her hair with her hand. "Yes, well, I'm sorry, sir, but you know how the Americans can be. I have the hardest job of anyone," her voice raised an octave, pleading her case.

The elderly man slowly twisted his five-carat diamond ring and pursed his lips. "Yes, the Americans. They have always been a challenge. Yet regions have folded much quicker than I thought." He smiled. "I brought down two towers, and they threw away some freedom like that." He snapped his fingers, and the people in the screens chuckled in agreement. "What is the problem now? We've been molding their minds in schools now since the 60s. Common Core has been in place in one form or another and should speed up the process now that we have implemented it fully and caught them unawares of its content. We control their culture with Hollywood, social media, the mainstream media, most of their universities, public education, and technology. There should be no more resistance. I should be controlling their minds and hearts by now."

The woman cleared her throat again, "Yes, sir. Parochial and homeschoolers are hard to get a firm grip on. And some people are still fighting Common Core. Some parents had to be arrested at school board meetings, which caused more people to question the content. The north and east states, California, and most of the Midwest are fine. It's the west and south that I'm having the most trouble with."

The man had absentmindedly picked up a teabag. He crushed it in a rare show of uncontrolled anger and flung it across the room. "This has gone on long enough. You will issue an executive order that all teachers who do not follow the revised Common Core curriculum word for word will be under house arrest and have their teaching license removed. You will also issue an executive order that there will be no more protests."

The woman nervously patted her hair. "But, sir, the First Amendment states—"

The man slammed his fist on the desk, making everyone jump. "I don't want to hear about the Constitution! We got rid of cursive writing so they won't be able to read the original document. We rewrote its content in their textbooks. We chipped away at their heroes. They shouldn't even remember their rights!"

"Yes, sir, that part is going well. But the adults still remember and are teaching their children. It will take a generation or two to die out."

"No! No, I want to be the one to see the fruits of our labor," the elderly man pursed his lips and squinted his eyes in concentration. "So… so the family is still the problem." He glanced to his left as if listening to someone, slowly nodding his head from time to time. No one in the screen dared to break the silence. "Yes… we have broken the family with lust and drugs and financial problems, but it is time for the final stroke. It is time to fully implement the government housing across the country and destroy the family. You must take all of the children away from their parents and have them raised by the government."

The woman sucked in her breath. "But… sir, how can I do that?"

The man glanced to his left and sneered. "Easily. Call in loans in Small Town, USA, so even more people lose their homes, bulldoze those houses, and get them in the new government dormitories. It worked well in the major cities. Build more structures and proclaim it in the name of job creation so the people welcome them. At the same time, increase the financial burden in the name of security. Increase the pressure on the small businesses and crush them once and for all so more people depend on the government. Increase the tax on gas. Make churches pay taxes in the name of "fair share" to close them. We need to crush this annoying morality. Set up bands of youth again and bring back the flash mobs. That should be easy. Many are already bored playing the video games we designed so they are ready to increase their violence lust and do it for real. Make them very violent, hit shopping malls and churches. Spray paint racial slurs. Stirring up racism is always beneficial to us. Feed the media story after story. The stress will make people join in the rioting. After a few months, they will beg for your help. You took away their guns in the name of security. They are defenseless against these homegrown terrorists." The man locked eyes with her. "You will be their savior once again."

A look of self-serving pride washed over her face. "Yes. Yes, once again you lead us well."

"Use the standardized tests as a gauge," the man continued. "Any student who doesn't succumb to our theology will be reeducated. Are the facilities ready?"

"Yes, sir."

The man leaned back in his leather chair contentedly. He listened to the reports from the other heads of state. They were far less dramatic. The other countries fell in line years before.

Chapter 3

Kaylee groaned then laughed as the dog covered her face with kisses. "OK, OK." She sat up in her bed. "Job number one today is to give you a bath. And give you a name. Hmm… how about Hero?" She stretched and yawned. "What a weird night last night. I hope whatever drug they slipped into my drink won't fry my brain permanently or—" Kaylee caught her breath and pulled her sheet up to her chin. "Oh, no. It's still happening."

Cotravin smiled and gave her a quick wave as he leaned against her desk. "Good morning."

Kaylee chewed her lip. She glanced around the room, and the cell phone on the nightstand caught her eye. She scooped it up and quickly texted Jordan *Was last night real?*

A moment later, her phone chimed, and she read ☺ *Yes, isn't he there?* She glanced up, and Cotravin shyly waved again. *Yes.*

"Ask him to meet us later. We need to talk," Cotravin said.

Can we meet later? She texted and waited.

Sure. Let's go to 11:30 Mass & then we can talk afterwards.

Cotravin stood up excitedly. His eyes pleaded. She went to Mass occasionally with Grammie, but she usually just dropped Grammie off and went to the Stacks restaurant and ate with Mandy until it was time to pick her grandmother up. Cotravin folded his hands in front of him like a little kid begging for ice cream. Kaylee rolled her eyes and texted *Sounds like a great idea. We can go to Stacks afterwards.*

Cotravin let out a whoop. "Didn't realize how much you liked pancakes," she teased. Kaylee got out of bed and went to her closet. She smiled; it made her feel good to make him so happy. She grabbed an outfit and almost ran into Grammie as she stepped into the hallway.

Grammie gave her a big hug, "I'm so happy you are coming to Mass!"

Kaylee glanced at the glow next to her grandma. "Big mouth," she joked.

Grammie held Kaylee's shoulders and followed her gaze. She slowly looked back at Kaylee. "Do you see my angel?"

"Sort of. More of a faint, blurry light for some reason," Kaylee studied the angel. "Are you a boy or a girl?" She waited for an answer. "Hello? You shy?"

Grammie laughed. "I think only I can hear her."

Kaylee glanced at Cotravin. "Why could I hear and see Fredouglass?"

Cotravin stood to her right. "You will only see the ones that are on the mission."

"Ooooh," Kaylee giggled. "Are we like secret agents or something?"

Cotravin looked at her seriously. "We will discuss this later, but do not make light of this. The last time this has happened in America was with Abraham... and George before that."

Kaylee tilted her head. "Let me guess. Washington?"

Cotravin nodded.

"Oh, boy." Kaylee was starting to worry about what she was getting involved in.

Grammie knitted her eyebrows in concern. "What is he saying?"

"Nothing, Grammie," Kaylee smiled reassuredly. "I better get into the shower if we are going to make it on time." She paused and looked at Cotravin. "You... you don't come in with me, do you? I mean, you're a guy."

Cotravin chuckled. "I'm always with you, but don't be alarmed. I don't look at you that way. I'm an angel, you are my beloved."

Kaylee smiled; she liked it when he called her beloved. "But still. You're a guy. Aren't you guys big on modesty? You kept yelling that last night." She brushed off Grammie's reaction. "No worries. Nothing happened last night."

"I'm not really a guy as you think of one."

Kaylee looked him up and down. "Really? You're a girl?"

"I'm neither physically. I have the basic shape of a human because you were based off of us. But angels are purely spiritual and don't need to reproduce so we don't have need for certain parts that humans do. Therefore, you humans generally refer to us as male or female because of certain qualities."

"Like your big biceps and cool hair?"

Cotravin smiled and nodded.

Kaylee twisted her lips. "Bummer. You would have made a really hot boyfriend."

Grammie playfully spanked her. "Goodness, the things you say. Off with you now."

Kaylee closed the door to the bathroom and started to undress then paused.

Cotravin laughed. "If it makes you more comfortable, I can fade out. I usually join the Choir of Praise during times like this and when you are sleeping. I'm with you if you needed me, but I'm concentrating somewhere else. Understand?"

Kaylee nodded. "Can you read my thoughts?"

Cotravin shook his head. "I am not the Lord. Only He can search the heart. St. Thomas Aquinas was quite right when he said that 'Therefore angels do not know the secrets of hearts.' But I can read your thoughts when you address them to me."

"But just now in the room, you followed my conversation with Jordan."

"I can read and hear all electronic conversations."

"Like the NSA," she joked.

Cotravin smiled.

Kaylee pondered this. "So—"

"Beloved," Cotravin gently coaxed, "I know you have many questions. But we mustn't be late for Mass. For even though our Lord is ever present with us, we have a special intimacy with Him at Mass that I crave."

Kaylee nodded and started to take off her pajamas then paused, raising her eyebrows at him. Cotravin shook his head, a bit annoyed, and faded into a faint light. "Thank you."

As they walked down the aisle, Kaylee enjoyed watching Cotravin's reaction. He was bursting with happiness, glowing so brightly that she was surprised it didn't hurt her eyes. She noticed small spots of light about the size of a tennis ball on the right shoulder of everyone present. She spotted Jordan, who was waving them over. She guided Grammie to the pew.

"Hi," she greeted Jordan. "Grammie, you remember Jordan?"

"The deacon's son, my, yes," Grammie grasped his hand warmly and sat down.

Jordan slightly bowed to Cotravin. Kaylee hastily imitated him and bowed towards Fredouglass. Both angels glowed brighter, obviously appreciating the gesture. As Mass started, Kaylee started to glance around the room. *What is that girl thinking with that hair?* She slightly giggled at her own joke and then caught Cotravin's glare. Intimidated, even with his small size on her shoulder, she sat up straighter.

"Pray to have an open heart and mind for Mass. Then you will grow to love and appreciate the gift," he scolded.

Kaylee sighed and closed her eyes. She prayed as Cotravin instructed. When she opened her eyes, she was surprised to find that she did pay more attention. When Jordan's dad rose to read the Gospel, she exchanged glances with Jordan, who was obviously proud. His dad stayed at the pulpit and began his homily.

"It isn't easy being a Christian today. We are mocked openly. For those of us with a bit of frosting in our hair," there was a chuckle through the congregation, "This isn't the America we remember as children. But today's readings clearly show us that we have the duty to fight against the worldly desires of our culture and teach our children the Truth or all will be lost. Make no mistake. We are in a daily battle." Jordan's dad continued to speak. Kaylee had an uneasy feeling that his words were truer for his son and her than he realized.

Kaylee followed the crowd… standing, kneeling, sitting, and fumbling through the responses as much as she could remember. As she stood in the Communion line, the look of anticipation on Cotravin's innocent face actually started to make her nervous.

The pastor looked at Kaylee and held up the host. "The body of Christ."

"Amen," Kaylee agreed. She was about to absently pop it in her mouth when she looked at Cotravin and paused. He had a look of such adoration, such love, such devotion as he stared at the host that he actually brought tears to her eyes. She glanced up at the huge crucifix over the altar, suddenly realizing how unworthy she was yet was still being called to His table. The impatient parishioner behind her in line cleared his throat. She moved to the cup, drowning in emotion. She placed the host reverently in her mouth. Cotravin gasped in pure ecstasy.

"Blood of Christ," the Eucharistic minister held out the beautifully crafted gold chalice.

Kaylee took the chalice, "Amen," and sipped it, slightly shaking as a tear rolled down her face. She gave the cup back to the minister who gave her an odd look. She wiped another tear from her eye when she knelt down to pray as the others went up for Communion.

Cotravin beamed, "I told you the prayer would help."

Kaylee felt a bit vulnerable, knowing a familiar part of her just died and another uncharted one was beginning. The choir sang "Strength for the Journey." She stared at the people as they whispered "Amen" and took the Eucharist. Some seemed to be having the same experience as she had; most just absently took it and went through the motions. How sad. She was one of them just moments before.

The Mass continued and then the pastor gave the congregation the final blessing. Jordan's dad smiled and directed, "Go in peace and serve the Lord by your lives."

Kaylee stopped the car in front of her house. Jordan quickly got out of the backseat, opened Grammie's door, and helped her out. Grammie winked at Kaylee and gushed over Jordan's manners. He waved to her as he got into the passenger seat.

"You realize she wants us to get married now."

Jordan looked at her in surprise as Kaylee pulled away and navigated to Stacks.

"We conferenced with Mikha'el while you slept," Fredouglass began. "It is as we thought. The Fallen are making a major move to destroy the American Covenant."

"There's an American Covenant?" Jordan asked.

"Yes," Cotravin answered. "Mikha'el said an instructor will be revealed tomorrow."

"Who?" inquired Kaylee.

"We don't know yet," Cotravin answered.

"Can't you guys look into the future or something?"

Fredouglass frowned. "Only the Almighty can see the future."

"Well, then how do we know there will be an instructor tomorrow?"

"Because the Almighty told Mikha'el who then told us."

"Who are the Fallen?"

"The angels who followed Lucifer before creation," Fredouglass answered impatiently.

"Peace, Brother," Cotravin gently placed his hand on Fredouglasss's arm. "She speaks out of ignorance, but she will learn."

Kaylee cringed. This must all be a mistake. Why would she be chosen to do some heavenly mission?

Mandy hugged her as they walked up to the hostess stand. She raised her eyebrows up and down when Kaylee asked for a table for two. "Follow me, monsieur and mademoiselle," she said in a French accent.

As they sat down in the booth, a middle-aged man walked out of the office and harshly pushed through the door leading into the kitchen.

"What's up with your dad?" Kaylee asked.

Mandy stared worriedly at the door her father used and sighed, "More bad news. We are barely holding on to keep this place going."

Jordan scanned the room. "Really? You guys are always packed."

Mandy exhaled, "I know. But every time we turn around, there are more regulations and taxes…" She brought her attention back to the table. "Listen to me sounding like a gloom and doom grown-up. So… what's the deal with you two? First a mysterious pickup last night and now a cozy brunch."

Jordan blushed and started to fumble with the lazy Susan filled with different flavors of syrup.

"Menus, please, miss," Kaylee narrowed her gaze to warn her friend.

"Mmm-hmm, right away," Mandy handed them the menus she was holding. She mouthed *call me later* to Kaylee and went back to work.

"Too bad about her family's restaurant," Jordan commented as he scanned the menu.

"It's part of the evil plan," Cotravin stated.

"What plan?" Kaylee asked, ignoring the menu, because she always got the same thing. "If they go after waffles and pancakes, that is very evil."

Cotravin smiled, enjoying her playfulness momentarily and then got serious. "Financial worries make America very vulnerable."

"And moldable," Fredouglass answered.

"You guys make it sound like a global conspiracy, like the guy on cable that Grammie watches," Kaylee laughed.

"Yes," the angels chorused.

"You aren't saying that we are supposed to fight *that*, are you?" Jordan sputtered.

"Mikha'el has not revealed that far into the plan," Fredouglass offered. "But yes."

"It is always your choice, Beloveds," Cotravin comforted them. "But you have surely been called to fight in a battle of great importance. Mikha'el said this was to make a final stand for America's soul, for America's liberty." Kaylee and Jordan stared at him with their mouths dropped. "God is on your side so whom shall you fear? But it is your choice whether or not to fight."

"I know. A big decision," Mandy walked up to them and took the pencil from behind her ear. Kaylee and Jordan shifted their gazes to her, mouths still dropped in disbelief. "Oh, for Pete's sake, it's just brunch. Well?" They continued to stare at her, dumbfounded. She grabbed their menus. "Two Liberties, coming up." And she walked away.

Jordan looked at Kaylee.

"The Liberty is a waffle with strawberries, blueberries, bananas, a scoop of vanilla ice cream, and whipped cream," Kaylee softly explained, still stunned by the angels' revelation.

"Oh, sounds good," Jordan answered, equally stunned. "Liberty is good."

Chapter 4

Kaylee kept glancing at the clock on the wall. She could hardly concentrate on what her teacher was saying.

"Your paper should be easy to write," the young first-year teacher crossed her pretty legs as she sat on the stool in front of the class. "I simply want a two-page paper on how much better our society functions now that the Christian religion has been kicked out of the mainstream."

Kaylee was startled. She looked at Cotravin. He was scowling at the teacher with his arms folded in front of him. She slowly raised her hand.

"Yes, Kaylee?" The young teacher adjusted her trendy glasses.

"What if we don't believe that?"

"I'm sorry? I don't understand your question."

"What if we don't think society is better because Christianity has been kicked out of the mainstream?"

The teacher laughed heartily. "Oh, Kaylee, you are so funny. Of course you do." The smile slowly faded from her face, replaced by a menacing look. "Only an uneducated idiot still clings to an outdated religion that was only created to keep people in their place and deny women the rights to their own bodies. You're not an idiot, are you?"

There was an uncomfortable silence as the two females locked eyes, neither blinking. Some people shifted in their chairs. Several breathed an audible sigh of relief when the bell rang. Kaylee gathered her books, not breaking her stare. The teacher looked down when Kaylee reached the door.

"I look forward to reading your paper, Kaylee. It is worth twenty percent of your grade," the teacher barely veiled her threat.

Kaylee stopped and faced her. She smiled, "I guarantee it will blow your mind." She turned on her heel and left the room. The hallway was crowded and loud so she wasn't even noticed when she spoke aloud. "Looks like I'm going to fail that class," she huffed.

"Grades are not as important as keeping to the truth." Cotravin hovered above her right shoulder in his smaller version.

"I also noticed there was no light by her shoulder."

Cotravin nodded. "We cannot stay when we are not wanted. She made up her mind to go against the Way." He sighed. "But her Guardian Angel watches from afar in case she repents. There is always a chance, always hope."

Kaylee considered this. "Her angel can't make her be good?"

Cotravin slowly shook his head. "The Almighty gave humans free will. You choose every day until you stand before Him after your last breath. We merely guide and help you along the journey. The more you listen, the more we can help."

"You don't have free will?"

"Yes, but we chose long ago. That's why we who stayed are sinless. We are finished with temptation just as you will be when you go Home."

Kaylee returned Mrs. Whitman's greeting and slipped into her desk. She felt the most comfortable in this classroom. The desks were set up in a U shape to actually encourage discussion. Darius came in the room and gave the teacher a high five. He caught Kaylee's eye and sheepishly sauntered over to her desk.

He put his books down on the desk next to hers and cleared his throat. "Umm, look, I'm sorry about the party. We cool?"

Kaylee playfully punched his developed bicep, "Yeah, we're cool."

Darius gave a heavy sigh of relief. This class didn't have a seating chart, but Mandy was surprised when Jordan beat her to her usual seat on the other side of Kaylee and sat down. Mandy raised her eyebrows up and down while sitting in the desk in front of Kaylee. Kaylee blushed as she exchanged greetings with Jordan, and they both subtly bowed to the other's angel.

The bell rang, and the students quickly gave their full attention to Mrs. Whitman. She was well respected among them in spite, or perhaps because, she was the most challenging teacher on staff. She always pushed them to think. She had been teaching history for twenty-two years and really knew her material. She also had a motherly way about her that engaged the students.

"And now what you've all been waiting for," Mrs. Whitman patted the pile of paper on her desk. "The chance to discuss the importance of the Fourth Amendment." There was a playful groan from the students as she passed out the packets. "And why is it important to know these Bill of Rights?"

"Because if we don't know our rights, how will we know when they are being violated," Darius announced. The class chuckled, remembering Darius's story from the party.

"Quite right, Mr. King," Mrs. Whitman walked around the inside of the U as she spoke. "Miss Lincoln, would you be so kind as to read aloud the Fourth Amendment?"

"The right of the people to be secure in their persons, houses, papers, and effects, against unreasonable searches and seizures, shall not be violated," Mandy was interrupted by the classroom door opening. Four men and a woman entered the room. Three of the men were wearing identical blue suits and squinted as they scanned the room. Mrs. Whitman visibly straightened in recognition of the adults and offered them a strained smile. She nodded to Mandy to continue. "And no warrants shall issue, but upon probable cause, supported by oath or affirmation, and particularly describing the place to be searched, and the persons or things to be seized."

The adults stood against the wall and folded their arms.

"Thank you, Miss Lincoln," Mrs. Whitman continued, "and who can explain what this means?"

A student raised her hand, and Mrs. Whitman nodded at her. "It means that police and the government can't just come into our homes for no reason. They have to have a warrant signed from a judge for a particular thing they are looking for."

Another student raised his hand. "It's to prevent the government from invading our privacy. As you always say, the government serves us; we don't serve the government."

"That is enough," the first man bellowed. The class was startled. "Mrs. Whitman, I have been informed that you have been warned about this many times."

"What seems to be the problem?" Mrs. Whitman stood by her stool.

"You know very well what the problem is," the woman chimed in. "You are to stick to the curriculum and that's all. Mr. Reid is from the *federal* Department of Education."

"All the way from Washington DC? My, my," Mrs. Whitman pondered mockingly. "How did you find your way here to little ol' Arlington Heights, Illinois?"

"I reported you," the woman lifted her nose, giving her an arrogant air about her. "As a school board member, I have an obligation to make sure the curriculum is followed."

"I found the curriculum…" Mrs. Whitman smiled, "lacking in this area. This is supplemental material. Surely there is nothing wrong with exposing the students to our Constitution. The Constitution is still the law of the land, is it not?" she challenged.

"The law of this land is the elected president, not some dusty piece of paper that was written by some old white men hundreds of years ago."

"Actually, most of them were in their twenties and thirties," Mrs. Whitman corrected. "And what you just said is treason."

"Not important," the woman continued. "But what is important is the education of these students. We will not stand by as you go rogue on the curriculum."

"I hardly think teaching about the Constitution is—"

"You leave us no choice," Mr. Reid stated. "Arrest her."

One of the men wearing a blue suit stepped forward and grabbed Mrs. Whitman's left arm. She was stunned, so he easily handcuffed her hands behind her back before she could react. The class erupted in protest, several students rising to their feet.

Darius rushed to Mrs. Whitman's side. "Get away from her!" He stepped between her and the man, equal to his large frame. "You have no right!"

Mr. Reid mockingly held up a piece of paper. "Actually, we do, young man. This teacher is in violation of an executive order."

"This is stupid!" Darius protested. "She's not teaching anything bad!"

"We will decide what is good and bad to teach," Mr. Reid said in a condescending tone. "After all, we are the professionals."

"This is outrageous!" Mrs. Whitman cried. "I'm the president of the teacher's union and know you can't do this! We have rights in place to protect us from crazy bureaucrats like you who know nothing of teaching in the classroom. You sit around in your fancy offices and could care less about our students or their academics. You've gone too far!"

"Obviously, not far enough," Mr. Reid calmly argued, "or we wouldn't have to deal with teachers like you—dinosaurs still clinging to the good ol' days. No matter. We just passed a law thanks to your cooperating national union to ensure that the teachers that we have trained will be the only ones in your precious classrooms molding the minds of your precious students." He grinned. "All in the name of budget costs."

The group of adults sneered when they saw horror register on Mrs. Whitman's face. The students were getting louder. Mr. Reid motioned to the other man in a blue suit, who promptly stepped forward and pulled out a gun.

"Enough!" He was greeted with instant silence. The students slowly sat down except for Darius, who froze, standing next to his teacher.

"What in God's name are you doing?" Mrs. Whitman breathed.

"Actually," Mr. Reid scoffed, leaning close to her, "haven't you heard? God isn't allowed in public schools anymore."

Kaylee's heart was beating hard in her chest. Cotravin stood in front of her in his full size. She noticed he now wore some kind of white armor on his chest and arms. Fredouglass had the same posture in front of Jordan. She noticed that some of the students had a light blazing in front of them. The five intruding adults lacked any light around them.

"Children," the woman's voice was eerily sweet as she stood next to the man with the gun. She motioned to the young man in the shirt and tie. "This is Mr. Bennedict. He will be your teacher from now on. Have a good day."

The man in the shirt and tie started to gather the packets and smiled as if nothing was out of the ordinary. "OK, my name is Mr. Bennedict as they said, and we will just get rid of this garbage."

The man in the blue suit pushed Mrs. Whitman roughly towards the door. She slightly resisted but was no match for his size. Darius stepped forward but stopped as the other man in the blue suit aimed his gun straight at Darius's chest. Mrs. Whitman charged towards them but was pushed up against the wall, knocking down a Common Core poster that had "End all bullying" in large letters.

"Wait, please," she begged as a tear rolled down her cheek. "Please don't hurt them. I'll go, I'll go."

Darius shook his head and reached out his hand. He froze again as the man with the gun sneered in a sinister way, still aiming at him.

"But, Mrs. Whitman," Darius's voice was quivering, "you taught us that the only way evil can win is if good people did nothing. 'Give me liberty or give me death' and all of that."

She gave him a motherly smile, "Yes, Darius, but even George Washington knew when it was best to retreat. Live to fight and win another day."

Another tear ran down her cheek as she was shoved out of the door. The other adults exited the room one by one. The man with the blue suit holding the gun towards Darius glared at him. Darius defiantly puffed out his chest and squared his shoulders.

"Hmph." The man turned and holstered his gun as he closed the door behind him.

"Well, that was exciting," chuckled Mr. Bennedict nervously.

Darius glowered at him, "What is wrong with you, dude?"

Mr. Bennedict cleared his throat, "Yes, well, time to get back to work. I'll just pass out our approved textbooks, and we will get started." Darius gaped at him in disbelief. "Young man, time to sit down now." The new teacher pushed Darius.

"Get your hands off of me, man," Darius warned, not moving.

The new teacher pushed a bit harder. "Come on now, or I will call the principal."

Darius clinched his teeth. He looked behind Mr. Bennedict, and his eyes fell on a picture of Mrs. Whitman with her family standing in front of the Martin Luther King Jr. monument. "No."

"What did you say?" Mr. Bennedict said forebodingly.

Darius locked eyes with him. "I said no! This is messed up, man! I'm not playing this game anymore!" He marched over to the desk, snatched the picture, and pointed to a Martin Luther King Jr. poster and read the quote. "The ultimate measure of a man is not where he stands in moments of comfort and convenience, but where he stands at times of challenge and controversy." He pushed the stack of government-approved history books on the floor and stalked out of the room. Kaylee looked at Cotravin for guidance. He nodded his head in unison with Fredouglass. Kaylee and Jordan scooped up their books and walked towards the door. Mandy and a few other students quickly followed.

"Wait! Wait!" Mr. Bennedict ordered. "You will all be suspended! Every one of you! I will report you!" He paused, desperate to stop them. "This will be on your record! You'll never get into college! Your lives will be ruined! Come back!"

Later that evening, Mrs. Whitman's doorbell rang. Her husband slowly opened the door, and a smile broke across his face. "Honey, it's for you."

"I don't want to talk to anyone," she sobbed from inside the house.

"Oh," his eyes welled with tears, "I think you'll want to speak to these visitors."

Mrs. Whitman appeared at the door, her eyes puffy and red from crying.

Kaylee, Jordan, Mandy, and Darius all stood on her porch.

Darius held out a bouquet of flowers. "We sort of got suspended for a few days. Know anybody who could tutor us?" Mrs. Whitman slowly took the flowers. "They can stop you from being a teacher at our school, but they can't stop you from teaching us."

Mrs. Whitman had tears running down her face, but this time from happiness. She quickly gathered the teens in a group hug.

"The instructor is revealed," Cotravin said, folding his arms over his armor.

Fredouglass nodded. "The next step begins."

Chapter 5

Weeks passed with the same pattern. They went to school, did homework, ate dinner, and met at Mrs. Whitman's home for the real history lessons.

Darius rang Kaylee's doorbell. Hero jumped up on him as he playfully rubbed his head, making it shake from side to side.

"This is a great dog," Darius laughed. "What is he? Looks like a mix of German Shepard and Golden Retriever… he's a German Retriever."

"A Golden Shepard," Cotravin smiled.

"Oh, brother," Darius rolled his eyes. "Even our dogs are holy now."

Darius drove Kaylee to Mrs. Whitman's house. They jogged up the porch steps and joined Jordan, who just rang the doorbell. Darius scooped up the jack-o'-lantern on the porch and held it in front of his face. A seven-year-old boy and nine-year-old girl answered the door. They screamed and laughed as Darius chased them into the house. Jordan took Kaylee's jacket and hung it up in the front closet.

Mulana, Darius's angel, smiled lovingly at him as he yelped from burning his mouth on the hot apple cider. She had flowing hair that looked like ebony silk and was, of course, stunningly beautiful. Mandy greeted her warmly when she sat down next to Darius.

"Are you surprised that Darius's angel would be a gorgeous Asian girl?" Jordan poised as he hung up his own jacket. "Lucky."

Fredouglass folded his arms, pouting.

Kaylee giggled, and they joined the group.

"Mmmm," Jordan sipped from a mug that had "World's Best Teacher" on it.

As they all settled in, Mrs. Whitman aimed the remote and was about to turn off the news when a story caught her attention.

"Teachers are protesting the surprise decision for mandatory retirement of any teacher that has a teaching certificate over six years," the pretty news anchor stated. Mr. Reid came onto the screen, and Darius made a sound like a growl. "We regret this action but believe it is in the best interest of the taxpayers. The union left us no other choice."

Mrs. Whitman winced. "Our union worked with that guy to get things like Common Core going, thinking it was actually coming from the states. Now he reveals the real content that most of us object to, and he turned on us, using our benefits as the deathblow." She shook her head sadly. "We were just useful fools."

The news anchor appeared again, "In other news, there was another teen mob attack. This time in Ohio." Scenes of a shopping mall flashed on the big screen TV. "Six were reported killed, many more wounded. Due to this rise in violence, President Effluent has issued an executive order forbidding any religious decoration in public places or that can be seen from public sidewalks. This includes Christmas lights on private homes." The news went to a scene of President Effluent at the White House. "Of course, this will only be a temporary measure until this situation is under control. The flash mobs are obviously targeting holiday décor in the malls, so removing them will insure everyone's safety. Can any sane person say that twinkling lights and fancy evergreen swags are worth more than a person's life? Similarly, I have worked closely with Congress and have learned today that the Public Security and Reeducation Act has finally been passed. This new law ensures that all youths eighteen years or younger will be subject to mandatory reeducation in a federally run facility for any infraction of the law. We, as your government, have heard your cries to do something about the youth problem in America. If delinquent parents don't train their children to be respectful citizens so we can all live in a safe country, then our government will. I, as your president, always have your security as top priority."

Mrs. Whitman clicked off the TV.

"Can she do that?" Darius asked.

Mrs. Whitman patted the bulky ankle brace with a flashing light. "I can't believe they are doing a lot of things. I'm a prisoner in my own home for another month. And have now joined the masses of the unemployed." She tossed a paper in front of Kaylee. There was red ink with insulting comments and an F that covered half of the page as well as constructive comments and an A- written in green. "There's your real grade on your English paper. Nice job with your evidence. Too bad my green grade won't get factored into your grade point average."

Kaylee started to read through it. "Christmas colors," she observed. "You and Ms. Academin might get arrested. Too bad she won't be fired."

"Yes," Mrs. Whitman slowly shook her head, "she's exactly what they want molding the next generation. Speaking of which, where did we leave off?"

"George Washington just saw that his coat and hat had bullet holes in them but never got shot!" Darius said excitedly.

"Mmmm, yes," Mrs. Whitman smiled. "I like to leave you with a cliff-hanger so you'll come back. Here is a copy of primary documents of two different witnesses." She handed out the papers. "One is from a staff sergeant that was with George Washington, and the other is by an American chief who was firing at him."

"Cool, so you think that he was saved to lead America to victory?" Mandy scanned over the documents.

"You be the judges. There's much more evidence to support it. General Washington was very devout in reading the Bible and holding services for the troops."

"The new textbook taught us that he wasn't religious."

Mrs. Whitman rolled her eyes. "Again, you be the judges. But here are primary documents that talk of how General Washington would lead services himself if there was not a minister among them. He often quoted from Scripture in his speeches. And he required the troops to fast and pray before an important battle."

The discussion went on for a few hours. They examined pieces of evidence with every Founding Father and their desire to incorporate Christian/Judea values into the structure of the new country. The seven year old and nine year old fell asleep on Jordan's and Darius's laps respectively. They carefully carried them to bed, while the girls brought the dishes to the kitchen.

"Sorry we stayed past their bedtimes. Hope they won't be tired for school," Kaylee rinsed out the cups and put them in the dishwasher.

"We pulled them from school," Mrs. Whitman leaned against the counter.

"Really?"

She nodded. "There was another executive order. In the name of child safety, it is now required to put in a chip in the left shoulder under the skin of every child under twelve years old. If you refuse to, your child can't attend school. We refused. Plus, they were getting teased at school because of my situation."

"Well, the way things are going, they are much better off. Most of the teachers are getting replaced now with ones fresh out of school. If they are like the new teachers we have now, they are like robot teachers. It's kinda weird."

"That's true. But it's really just a gesture on our part, I guess. There was a leak reported that there is another law about to be passed that the chips will be mandatory for everyone twenty-five years and younger or you will have to pay a fine. And they are basically taxing nonpublic schooling, including homeschooling, so high that only the rich can afford not to comply."

Mandy walked to her car with Darius, while Jordan hung back with Kaylee on the porch as she put the jack-o'-lantern back in place.

"Umm, Kaylee," Jordan whispered, nervously adjusting his hat. She gave him her full attention. "I was wondering if you—and it's cool if you don't—but if you wanted to maybe go to the Homecoming Masquerade Dance with me."

Kaylee was surprised and looked at Cotravin. He and Fredouglass suddenly studied the ceiling of the porch like they weren't paying them any attention. She looked back at Jordan, who was waiting in obvious discomfort. She smiled, "Yes, that would be really great." Jordan beamed, while Cotravin and Fredouglass exchanged a high five.

As soon as Kaylee got in the passenger side of Darius's car, she texted Mandy *Jordan asked me to the dance!* Her phone chimed *Darius asked me!* Kaylee let out a happy squeal.

Darius rolled his eyes. "Well, that didn't take long."

Kaylee playfully punched his shoulder. "All four of us should go to the mall tomorrow after school to pick out matching masks!"

"Oh, yea," Darius moaned. "Shopping. Hooh-rah."

Kaylee noticed the Casting Crowns song on the radio. She gave Darius a questioning look.

"Oh," Darius mumbled. "Mulana didn't like the lyrics in most of the rap songs. This makes her happy."

"Mmm-hmm," Kaylee teased. "And I noticed you haven't had a cigarette, a beer, or sworn in a while."

"Yeah, well," Darius shifted in his seat. "When I know she's watching..."

Kaylee laughed. "I know what you mean." She smiled at him. "And Mandy thinks the new you is even hotter."

Darius beamed.

*****

The girls walked slightly ahead of the boys in the mall, giggling with Mulana and Darwallace, Mandy's angel. The angels' long hair flowing and glimmering.

"I don't care what you say, dudes," Jordan said to Fredouglass and Cotravin, "those angels are definitely all female."

There were many masks to pick from. They were fancy with feathers and faux jewels and different shapes. The girls kept trying them on and asking each other's opinions. Mulana and Darwallace eagerly participated. Jordan, Darius, Fredouglass, and Cotravin all leaned against the aisle bins with their arms folded.

"Jordan, I think you're right, dude," Darius observed. "Nothing brings out the female in one of God's creatures more than shopping."

"Do you like this one?" Kaylee and Mandy held up identical masks with splashes of purple, blue, and green with gold trim. There were fluffy feathers of the same colors that were sticking out of the right side and faux diamonds on the left. The boys gave them a thumbs up. The girls squealed, including Mulana and Darwallace.

"Yep," Cotravin and Fredouglass agreed, "female."

They paid for their masks and went out into the mall, noticing how many shops were vacant with "Available for rent" signs hanging on their closed gates. Suddenly, gunfire echoed. The four angels instantly wore white battle armor and looked around. The four teens ducked into the nearest shop called Pitter Patter.

Gunfire continued to sound as shoppers screamed and headed for the doors. As they neared the outside doors, a few shoppers fell with blood squirting from their bodies. Quickly, people stopped going in that dangerous direction and took cover.

Jordan dialed 911 and described the scene. "Are you kidding me?" He paused. "I don't care about budget cuts! People are dying!" He angrily hung up and looked at the group. "They might take a while."

"What the—" Darius was squatting but lifted up one foot.

A very pregnant woman hiding on the floor next to him started to cry.

"Lady, please tell me you just dropped a Mountain Dew."

"My water just broke," she sobbed.

"OK, OK, no problem," Mandy said, her voice quivering. "What did we learn in health class? Labor lasts hours, right? We'll be out of here, and you'll get to the hospital. No problem."

The woman moaned loudly. "I don't think so." She started her Lamaze breathing. "This is my fourth baby. The other ones were fairly quick. I'm lucky that way."

"Yep, lucky," Jordan rubbed his forehead.

Ten minutes later, she moaned loudly again. A shooter paused five stores away and started to come their way.

"We need to take out that shooter before he hurts anyone in here," Fredouglass said.

"I hope by 'we' you mean you invisible ones in our group," Darius whispered.

Fredouglass shook his head. "We only fight in spiritual battles."

"Remember George Washington's hat and coat?" Mulana offered.

"Can you protect me like that?"

"More or less," she shrugged. "I mean, don't go strolling out there walking up to the guy or anything."

Suddenly, the mall music got very loud and Bonnie Tyler's "I Need a Hero" blared.

Jordan looked at Darwallace, "Really?"

She smiled, "Mood music, lad. Helps give ya some moxy."

Darius sighed heavily as more shots rang out, very near. "Alright. We need a weapon."

Jordan glanced around and grabbed two umbrella strollers. Darius glared at him. "It's either these or those fluffy bunnies!"

They positioned themselves on each side of the entrance, holding a folded stroller like a baseball bat. The shooter had stopped a store away from them. Distant shots rang out, and he laughed. The minutes crawled by. The pregnant woman held a stuffed teddy bear to her face to stifle her moan, but the shooter heard her and stalked to the store. He slowly entered. Darius and Jordan swung as hard as they could and hit him in the face and abdomen simultaneously. Blood spurted from his nose as he fell backwards and hit the floor, his rifle sliding across the floor and stopping at Mandy's feet. She picked it up and aimed it at the shooter. He was dressed all in black.

"Thou shalt not kill," Darwallace warned.

"Are you kidding?"

"This isn't a video game." Darwallace continued. "Taking a life is very serious. Don't do it if ya don't have to."

Kaylee stood up quickly and grabbed some toddler leashes from the wall display.

Jordan quickly tied the shooter's hands and feet behind his back.

"Great job," Darius expressed.

"Junior rodeo champ."

The shooter started swearing at them, daring Mandy to shoot. Jordan grabbed a pink bunny and stuffed as much as he could in the shooter's mouth. "Angels do not like that kind of language, dude."

"There are three more," Fredouglass stated.

"The baby's angel said she is coming in about forty minutes," Mulana exclaimed.

"What?" Darius looked panicked. "Can't you tell her to stop? Just tell the baby to cool it."

"Look, buddy," the pregnant woman spat between heavy breathing, "I'm not exactly thrilled about this either!" She moaned and went into her breathing.

"It doesn't work that way," Mulana responded to Darius.

"Here comes another shooter," Cotravin informed.

"How close?" Kaylee asked.

"About twenty feet away, standing by the food court."

Kaylee grabbed a Johnny-jump-up and gave each boy one of the straps. She snatched a heavy metal piggy bank from the display table. "Hold tight." She pulled the seat back like a sling shot. She adjusted until she thought the aim was right. She looked at Cotravin, "Can you help with the aim?" He nodded. She pulled the seat back as far as the straps would stretch and let it go. The metal piggy bank flew out of the store and hit the other shooter in the head. He dropped to the floor, knocked out. The teens cheered then covered their mouths. Jordan and Darius scurried to the shooter and hog-tied him too.

Shots rang out, and a napkin container on the table by Jordan's head exploded. Darius and Jordan ducked and crawled quickly to the ice cream counter and swung over. The third shooter ran towards the counter with the rifle aimed. As he reached the counter, Jordan sprayed whipped cream from a nozzle in his face, while Darius threw cans of caramel. The shooter dropped the rifle and screamed in pain. The boys leaped over the counter and wrestled him to the ground. Mandy ran over with a couple more toddler leashes.

"What are you doing?" Darius bellowed. "You could get killed!"

"Oh, and you can't?"

Glass from the ice cream counter flew into the air as bullets shattered it. Mandy ducked behind a seven-foot plant. She followed the boys as they zigzagged around tables and reached the end of the food court. Several people were huddled in various hiding spots, most of them were middle schoolers and high schoolers.

"Luckily, this happened on a weeknight," Mandy gasped. "Not a ton of people."

"We need to see if we can sneak back to Kaylee," Jordan peered around the corner.

"It's clear," Fredouglass clarified.

The three of them made a run for it. They were two stores away when shots rang out. They dove into the Storyland store. They waited and listened for several minutes. Darius grabbed a pair of moose antlers and put them on.

Jordan rolled his eyes. "Seriously?"

"Hey," Darius replaced Jordan's cowboy hat with a jester's hat that had drooping ears. "If we are going to die, this is a happy place to do it."

"Don't get cocky because we are protecting you," Mulana warned. "You can still get hurt."

"We need weapons," Jordan scanned the store.

"Ooh, swords," Darius grabbed some swords and threw one to Jordan while taking one for himself. "Excalibur!" He pressed a button and lights twinkled up the blade.

"They're plastic!" Jordan complained.

"How are we supposed to do this? We aren't heroes!" Mandy demanded.

"The Almighty always picks the weak and unlikely to be His heroes," Fredouglass casually stated as he looked out the store window.

"To be sure," Darwallace agreed, "I'm impressed yer all still breathing yet."

"Yes," Mulana agreed. "You all are doing surprisingly well so far."

The three teens exchanged troubled looks.

"I mean, by all accounts, you should all be toes up, but here you are still slinging mud!" Darwallace beamed.

"Is this your idea of a pep talk?" Darius swallowed.

The angels looked at each other baffled.

"Don't be afraid, laddy," Darwallace softened her voice. "Yer all doing fine fer yer first battle. Some don't make it through, and there's no shame in that either. There would be a big reception in yer honor fer fighting fer the Almighty. So winning the battle today to move on to other battles or dying and having the reception today, either way, it will be grand."

The angels smiled and nodded their heads supportively.

Jordan held up his hand. "Please stop. Your pep talks are terrifying."

The angels exchanged perplexed looks as the shooter stepped into the store.

Jordan sprang up. He and Darius started dueling with the shooter. The shooter was startled at first but then aimed his rifle. Darius and Jordan managed to keep hitting the rifle sideways so the shooter could not get a clear shot. They backed up as he advanced. Suddenly, Mandy popped out from behind a table and smashed a basketball-sized snow globe on his head, knocking him to the ground with water and glitter splashing everywhere when it broke.

"That'll be $129.99, sir," Mandy stood over him with her hands on her hips.

Jordan grabbed a Jack in the Beanstalk jump rope and tied him up.

Mandy looked around. "I always liked this store." She took a purple plastic princess tiara and put it on her head.

"We're done shopping," Darius grabbed her hand. "Let's get out of here."

"All is clear!" Jordan called out. "You're safe! All is clear!"

People slowly started to emerge from hiding places and run for the exit doors. The teens heard a loud yell from Pitter Patter. They exchanged looks and then ran towards it. When they entered the store, Kaylee was kneeling between the pregnant woman's bent knees. Baby blankets surrounded the woman's legs; wet baby towels tossed to the side. Kaylee had also positioned a three-foot teddy bear behind the woman so she could lean against the wall a bit more comfortably.

"Where have you been?!" Kaylee yelled.

They stepped towards them.

"Get out!" shouted the woman. She moaned again and panted heavily.

The teens took a step back.

"Come here and help me!" Kaylee screamed.

"I—I don't know who to listen to," Jordan said helplessly.

"You two get out, Mandy come help me!"

"Now that's a great idea!" Darius agreed.

Jordan and Darius paced outside the Pitter Patter and watched as people were leaving. Lights flashed outside, and ten police officers walked in with their guns drawn.

"Well, welcome to the party, boys," Jordan sighed. Darius chuckled.

The police officers spread out, two coming towards them with their guns pointing forward.

"Police! Get your hands up!"

"Are they serious?"

"Now!" One of the policemen screamed. "Now!"

"Whoa, whoa," Jordan and Darius raised their hands.

The policeman frisked each of them, while his partner held a gun on them.

Jordan laughed. "Sorry, I'm ticklish."

"They're clean," the policeman reported.

The pregnant woman screamed. The police officers were startled and quickly pointed their guns in the direction of the store entrance.

"Trust us," Darius said, his hands still raised. "You do not want to go in there."

An officer entered.

"Get out!" the woman shrieked.

The officer backed out quickly, dragging the hog-tied shooter.

"Told you," Darius put down his hands.

The boys pointed out where the other shooters were. The officers wrote down details. The other officers were getting information from other witnesses. The boys fidgeted nervously.

"Warm water would be helpful for the girls if you want to be helpful," Mulana smiled.

Jordan and Darius jumped up gratefully and went to Pottery Mart, took a couple of large bowls, filled them with water from the restrooms, and brought them to the girls. They sat on the floor outside of the store for ten minutes.

A baby's cry rang out. The boys exchanged looks and slowly walked into the store. Mandy gently wiped the sweat off of the woman's face with several soft baby washcloths, while Kaylee carefully cleaned the baby with the water and then wrapped her in a baby blanket. She carefully handed the baby over to the woman, and the three of them laughed and cried together, bonding as the baby's Guardian Angel swooned over her.

Emergency personnel flooded the mall, blue and red lights dancing across the area. Jordan stepped out of the store and whistled, motioning one of the paramedics over. They waved to the woman as she was wheeled out on a gurney, holding the baby tenderly. It took about another hour before they were allowed to leave after telling their story many times.

"Wait!" Darius ran into the Pitter Patter and picked up their bags with the masks. "I'm not about to go shopping for these again."

"Thou shalt not steal," Fredouglass said as they passed the Storyland store. The teens stepped over the broken swords and snow globe and carefully replaced the hats they wore.

Darius held Mandy, and Jordan held Kaylee close as they stepped passed the four covered bodies by the exit doors. Their adrenalin was wearing off so the gravity of the past few hours crashed down on them.

"They could have been us," Mandy cried.

"No," Cotravin stated, "It is not your time. You have more to do."

Chapter 6

The angels abruptly stood alert in their full size, startling Kaylee, Mandy, Darius, and Jordan as they copied notes from the whiteboard in Mr. Bennedict's class.

"Be ready," Cotravin warned.

"Do not be afraid," Mulana commanded.

"God is with you," Darwallace reminded them.

"The battle continues," Fredouglass flexed, and he suddenly wore his white armor. The other angels followed, ready for combat.

Police officers and the principal entered the classroom. Alarm scattered across all of the students' faces. Mr. Bennedict walked over to the adults. "How may I help you?"

"These officers are here to arrest Kaylee Jefferson, Jordan Coolidge, Mandy Lincoln, and Darius King."

There was a collective gasp from the students. The four teens slowly stood as every student's eyes were on them.

"We have a right to know on what charge," Jordan demanded.

"Destruction of property," an officer announced as the four officers moved towards them.

"What property?" Mandy's voice quivered as an officer hand-cuffed her hands behind her back.

"Inventory at Pitter Patter, the Storyland Store, and Pottery Mart," another officer cuffed Kaylee.

"We delivered a baby!" Kaylee explained, exasperated.

"And took down four gunmen!" Darius added. Several teens applauded.

"Tell it to the judge," the officer roughly handcuffed Darius. "You punks need to learn that we uphold the law, not you."

The officers led them towards the door.

"Hmph," Mr. Bennedict clearly showed his disdain. "I'm not surprised. They are always bucking the system."

An officer recited the Miranda Rights as students and teachers gawked at the teens. "You have the right to remain silent. Anything you say will be used against you in a court of law. You have the right to an attorney during interrogation; if you cannot afford an attorney, one will be appointed to you."

"Tell Grammie," Kaylee whispered after they were seated in the two squad cars.

"And my dad," Jordan added.

Cotravin and Fredouglass nodded. They both concentrated momentarily. "Their respective angels have been notified. They will contact the other parents since they don't hear their angels."

A tear rolled down Kaylee's face as a policewoman took their fingerprints and mug shots. An officer took their belongings, including their cell phones, and put them in yellow envelopes. There were two holding cells about forty by forty feet each. One cell was filled with huddled children; the other with hardened adults making fun of them and reaching for them through the bars.

"Wait," the arresting officer pointed to the adult cell, his partner paused as he was about to unlock the children's cell. "Put them in that one." He leaned close to Jordan and hissed, "How do you like that Mr. I-have-rights?"

The four of them winced as the iron door slammed shut, imprisoning them. The holding cell's occupants looked their way, forty unfriendly eyes. Mandy cried into Darius's shoulders as he pulled her close. Jordan put a protective arm around Kaylee. They backed up against the bars by the children's cell.

"Well," Kaylee tried to sound lighthearted. "Grammie was arrested in the '60s, protesting in support of Civil Rights. Now we both have a record."

A twelve-year-old girl on the other side of the bars started hiccupping from crying so intensely. Kaylee was moved with pity for her.

"Hey," Kaylee engaged gently. "Hey, it's going to be OK. My name is Kaylee, what's yours?"

"B-B-Bailey G-G-Gates."

"Hi, Bailey," Kaylee talked soothingly, like her mom used to do when she came home crying from being bullied at school. "I bet your parents are waiting for you, and you'll be home in your own bed in no time."

Bailey looked at her hopefully. "D-d-do you really th-th-think so?"

"Sure," Kaylee smiled. "I doubt you robbed a bank or anything."

Bailey's smile revealed braces. "No. I got in trouble because I wanted my teacher to give me a grade on my paper."

Kaylee knitted her eyebrows. "That's all?"

Bailey started to tremble. "We aren't supposed to g-g-get grades anymore so kids d-d-don't feel bad about themselves. I-I-I just wanted to know if I did w-w-well on it. I used to be a straight A s-s-student. My old teacher liked it when I did extra research projects. But with this new teacher, I always get in t-t-trouble when I want to do well." She wiped her eyes. "She says I need to be reeducated."

A man sauntered over, reeking of cheap vodka and body odor. "What are you kiddies in for? Did you park your tricycles in a red zone?" The other occupants laughed. "You two sure are pretty. Want to dump the juniors and be with a real man?" The other inmates hooted and hollered.

Jordan and Darius protectively pushed the girls behind them and squared their shoulders.

"Wait," cautioned Fredouglass. "A fight is unwise."

"Stand firm," added Darwallas. "Another course is about to present itself."

"Now you know those girls wouldn't know what to do with a real man like yo'self," a scantily clothed girl in her twenties stepped between him and the teens. The dark smoky light on her left shoulder began to fade as the faint light on her right shoulder grew a little brighter. "They'd be a waste of yo' time."

The man turned his attention to her and roughly pulled her close. "But you sure know what to do with a real man, don't ya?" He licked her cheek.

The girl clenched her teeth briefly then said, "You know I do. Only cost you fifty dollars."

"Hmph," the man let her go. "You should pay me fifty dollars." And the other inmates laughed and congratulated him on such a witty comeback line when he ambled back over to them.

She looked fiercely at the teens. "Stop that crying, don't talk to anyone, and don't make eye contact." She casually went back to her place and sat down.

"Do not be afraid," Cotravin coaxed, "the Almighty protected Moses from Pharaoh, David from Goliath, Joseph from his brothers, the Founding Fathers from the king... He is protecting you now. Just believe, no matter what happens. He uses trials to bring His kingdom."

The four teens sat on the crowded dirty benches when their legs couldn't stand anymore. The smell of old sweat and urine stung their noses. Roaches crawled over the filthy floor. The room was drab and depressing; everything was a dull gray color. Everyone prayed silently.

After several hours, they were marched into a courtroom. Grammie and the parents stood anxiously. They sat for another couple of hours as the judge passed sentences on other youths. The bailiff pointed to a twelve-year-old boy on a bench wearing plastic bands for handcuffs and pushed him towards the public defender. The judge looked through his folder.

"Ahh," the judge sneered. "A troublemaker, eh? George Bambino, you were arrested for violating school rules for the endangerment of other students."

The public defender rubbed his eyes, exhausted from the night's proceedings. He could hardly keep up with all of the new regulations in the name of child safety. "He pleads guilty to bringing a bat and ball to school to play at recess, since the school banned sports for being such dangerous activities."

"Three months at the federal education facility." The judge banged his gavel.

"No!" A woman called out and was roughly escorted from the room.

The bailiff grabbed the next defendant by the shirt and dragged him over.

"You should know better than to threaten society with a gun," the judge reprimanded the six-year-old boy.

The boy was shaking, petrified. "But it was a toy Nerf gun."

"That doesn't matter!" The judge bellowed.

The public defender nudged the boy to be quiet. "He was in his own yard playing," the public defender stated as tears rolled down the child's face.

The judge slammed down his gavel. "One month in the reeducation program."

The bailiff roughly shoved the boy toward a big, red door. His parents protested as other guards held them back at gunpoint. The boy's lip trembled, the front of his pants stained with wetness, and with one last shove, he disappeared through the door.

"You've got to be kidding!" A man shouted as he stood up. "You're crazy! He's a young child! This is madness!"

"We have zero tolerance for people who disobey the strict gun laws." The judge smiled smugly. "Bailiff, put that man in a cell for disorderly conduct."

When it was the teens' turns, they stood before the judge.

"Well," he finished looking through the papers in front of him, "looks like you were busy."

The public defender looked quickly over his copy of the papers. "Yes, Your Honor, they were busy delivering a baby and saving countless lives by disarming four gunmen."

"And destroying hundreds of dollars' worth of merchandise in the process. They should have laid low until the proper authorities came."

"But, sir, we were trying to do that," Jordan exclaimed. "We called 911 and waited. But the baby started coming—"

"And the gunman came in the store—" Kaylee added.

"Because he heard the lady moan," Mandy put in.

"We had to do something, or we would have been killed," Darius finished.

The judge pounded his gavel. "I will have order in this court!"

The public defender gave them each a warning stare.

"Now, you have been charged with destruction of property and endangering the lives of others by taking the law into your own hands. How do you plea?" The judge looked at the teens.

"Not guilty, Your Honor," the public defender stated.

"I have read the official reports and find your actions to be reckless." The judge eyed each teen. "This isn't one of your video games where you go off half-cocked, trying to play the hero. You should have waited for the authorities. You can't go defending yourselves, or there would be anarchy. Your government is here to take care of you, so let it do its job. Our society cannot tolerate vigilantes. Under the new Public Security and Reeducation Act, I find you guilty and sentence you to one year in a federal reeducation program."

There was a loud gasp. The parents and Grammie clung to each other.

"Your Honor, please," Grammie begged.

"Of course, you can always appeal," the judge continued, "but that will be very costly. And in these trying times, who has the money?" He smiled. "Look on the bright side. These teens will be reeducated and, in a year, will come out respectful citizens. You can trust your government on that. You parents lack the skills needed to raise decent citizens and have obviously had a bad influence on these teens. Therefore, I do not regret informing you that you will not have any contact for the first six months of programming." The parents started shouting. "Take them into immediate custody and transport them to the Federal Youth Reeducation Facility in…" he adjusted his glasses as he looked at the tablet screen. "Oh, my, we are really filling these up. Looks like the closest one with openings is in Harrisburg, Illinois. Case dismissed." He banged his gavel. "Next case."

Officers started dragging the handcuffed teens toward a dark, red door. Other officers drew their guns, keeping the parents back. Grammie collapsed to the floor. Jordan's mom quickly tended her in the chaos.

"Grammie!" Kaylee shrieked, sobbing hysterically. "Grammie!" Cotravin zapped the guard and Kaylee broke free. She sprinted to

Grammie and dropped to the floor, holding Grammie's head in her lap.

Grammie shook as she brought a hand up to Kaylee's tear-streaked face. She tried to speak several times.

"What's wrong with her?" Kaylee sobbed.

"I think she's had a stroke, sweetheart," Jordan's mom gently placed a supportive hand on Kaylee's arm.

"L-L-Lazarus," Grammie struggled to get her words out. "Lazarus and… rich man."

"What?" Kaylee's vision was blurred with tears. "I don't understand."

"L-l-love you," Grandma stuttered.

"Don't do that," Kaylee choked. "Don't say goodbye to me."

Grammie's eyes fluttered, and her hand dropped.

"No!" Kaylee screamed. "No, Grammie, no!"

Grammie's eyes opened.

"Tell her you love her," Cotravin yelled, "Tell her now while you can!"

"I love you, Grammie!" Kaylee decreed. Grammie's eyes smiled at her. "I love you so much."

A guard wrapped his arms around her waist and pulled her up.

Then Grammie's eyes rolled to the back of her head.

"No!" Kaylee roared, "Grammie, please don't leave me! Grammie!"

The guards dragged the teens out of the courtroom. When they were in the hallway past the red door, they drew their guns.

"Enough of this drama!" One of the guards growled. "Now get walking towards that door at the end of the hallway and get on the bus!"

Kaylee's mind buzzed as the other three teens and angels tried to console her. She felt like she was floating down the hallway. Her mind couldn't absorb what was all happening. She couldn't understand what the guards were yelling at her, but it didn't really matter since they shoved her in the direction she was supposed to go. She stumbled on the stairs going into the bus. She scraped her shin on the metal step, not noticing the blood as it trickled down her leg. Cotravin gently guided her to a seat where a guard handcuffed her to a bar running along the wall of the bus. Their voices faded, sounding like they were under water. Thoughts assaulted her. How is Grammie? She doesn't deserve this. What will happen to me if she dies? Why does everyone in my life die?

"Beloved—" Cotravin began.

"Shut up." Kaylee stared blindly at the back of the dirty seat in front of her.

Cotravin was startled. "Beloved, I—"

Kaylee growled at him, "I said shut up! Go away and leave me alone!" She closed her eyes and leaned her forehead against the cold window. Louder and louder, she heard a gravelly voice whispering of the injustice; a voice that spoke of the poor way Grammie and she was treated by God.

The others gave up talking. There was just no consoling her. They all sat in silence for the four-hour bus ride. The only sound was the hum of the tires and the sniffling of crying children.

*****

A male nurse checked on Grammie's IV and wrote down the numbers from the monitor on his chart. "Don't worry. You'll be just fine with some physical therapy. It'll be no time at all. You'll see," he whispered to the unconscious Grammie. He walked down the hall, checking each of his patients.

A young nurse walked over to the head nurse. She tossed a chart on the head nurse's desk. The head nurse gave her a look of disapproval.

"Don't look at me that way," the young nurse shot back. "I don't make the decisions. The Health Distribution Panel does. And tonight we have four lucky winners."

"Winners, hmph," the head nurse did not hide her disgust. "Never thought I would live to see the day that bureaucrats play God on who lives and who dies in America."

"Well, it's not like I enjoy it," the young nurse stated. "But let's be realistic. There's only so much resources. We can't waste money. I mean, look… the ones tonight are a twenty-three year old in a severe motorcycle accident, a forty year old with lung cancer, a nine year old who needs a kidney transplant, and a seventy-seven year old lady who had a stroke. Do you know how much money their care would cost before the panels? Look on the bright side," the young nurse examined her nails. "There would have been five. But the older guy who needs the heart surgery has a son who's a congressman, so he gets the surgery instead of my magic needle."

The head nurse signed the chart and handed it back to the younger one, shaking her head in disagreement to the policy. The younger one walked down the hall into Grammie's room. She checked the chart and checked Grammie's information band on her wrist. She took out a syringe from her pocket and shot the drug into the IV tubing. She waited a moment and Grammie's unconscious body twitched. The monitor showed the heart beating slower and irregular, then the line went flat, and one long tone sounded until the young nurse clicked it off. She stared at Grammie.

"Not a bad way to go, really," she said to Grammie's corpse as she pulled the sheet over her face. "Sorry, but there's only so much money. You wouldn't want to waste all that money on physical therapy and treatment, would you? That's taking medical treatment away from someone who matters. I'm actually saving lives."

The patient in the next bed shuddered in horror, pretending to be asleep.

As the young nurse walked out of the room, the male nurse stopped in his tracks a few rooms away. He gasped and ran into Grammie's room. He covered his mouth and choked back a sob.

*****

"Beloved," Cotravin said gently. "I was just informed… Grammie went Home to the Lord."

Kaylee held her breath. Jordan, Darius, and Mandy all said words of condolences, wishing they could hug her instead of being handcuffed to their seats.

"Shut up!" Kaylee bellowed. "All of you just shut up! Especially you, Cotravin! I don't want to hear how much you or God loves me! Do I look loved right now? Does Grammie look loved right now? She worked hard all of her life! She taught in a Catholic school most of her life and barely got paid, let alone a decent pension! She suffered through the deaths of Grandpa and my parents! She went to Mass everyday! And for what? To have a stroke on a courtroom floor and die alone? No, no, no! This isn't love! This isn't right!"

"You are in danger! Don't send me away again!" Cotravin yelled, but he sounded as if he was far away. "A Fallen is at your side! Resist! Resist! Don't listen to his lies! Remember God never abandons you! He and I love you more than anything!"

Kaylee drowned out Cotravin's voice. She listened as the voice hissed in her ear. Grammie's stroke, the corrupt sentencing, almost getting killed at the mall, the senseless death of the four victims, the trouble at school, the abandonment of her father, the death of her mother... most of it started after Cotravin came into her life. She didn't deserve this. Grammie didn't deserve this. What is the point of following God if your life turns out like this?

"Go away, Cotravin," she mumbled. "I don't want you or God near me anymore."

Chapter 7

Kaylee refused to sit with her friends at mealtime or lecture time. Their daily schedule at the reeducation facility was monotonous; it started with the wake up buzzer at 5:30 a.m. They dressed in an orange jumpsuit, brushed their teeth and used the toilets in the group washrooms, ate one scoop of tasteless oatmeal, listened to a six-hour lecture, ate a tofu sandwich on dry white bread, did their assigned job, ate a cup of plain noodles with watery Kool-Aid, listened to another six-hour lecture, and then went to bed.

Kaylee was cleaning another toilet when someone came up behind her in the open stall. One person held her face in the water, while another pinned her body so she couldn't fight back. She gasped for air the few precious seconds they let her free of the water, and then they pushed her down again, crushing her face into the hard metal. She could hear them laughing. Her lungs burned and felt like they were going to explode if she didn't get fresh air soon. When she thought she was on the verge of passing out or dying, they suddenly released her. She sat up and gasped for air as her attackers left the bathroom. Mandy was kneeling on the floor next to her, crying as she wiped the blood from Kaylee's lip and forehead with the thin toilet paper. Kaylee pushed her away, not noticing that Mandy's eye was puffy and bruised.

The boys and angels whispered their fury when they joined them in the dinner line, vowing to pray harder for them, and professing they would be delivered soon. The boys had their own cuts and bruises. Kaylee simply walked away from them after the server dropped a scoop of overcooked noodles on her tray. She just didn't care anymore.

After a couple of weeks, the lectures were starting to make sense. They focused on how capitalism was run by evil men. The scratchy voice whispered to her, reminding her how poor Grammie was, how she struggled. The instructor went through American history, contradicting everything Mrs. Whitman taught them, saying how the Founding Fathers weren't on some noble cause but just wanted to be powerful. He showed pictures of dying Native Americans and described slaughter after slaughter. The raspy voice whispering in her ear emphasized the cruelty of it all as the instructor droned on.

Kaylee listened. The instructor was praising socialism, about how everything should be redistributed evenly, and how selfish the rich were in trying to fight the taxes that righted the wrong. Rich people. Rich people… rich men. Rich men? Kaylee started to remember something. She concentrated. What was it? Rich men? A rich man? Grammie! One of the last things Grammie said was something about a rich man. Kaylee made herself return to that horrible day in her mind's eye. She could picture Grammie laying in her arms. A rich man… and Lazarus.

At lunch, she sat down next to Mandy. They all started to say hello, excited to have her engage with them. She talked over them, not interested in what they were saying. She looked across the table at Jordan.

"What is the story of Lazarus and the rich man?" Kaylee demanded.

Jordan was staring at her left shoulder like he was watching a horror movie. "Kaylee, I just glimpsed something hideous on your left—"

"Jordan!" She exclaimed through clenched teeth so she didn't attract the guards' attention. "What is the story of Lazarus and the rich man?" The gravelly voice started to get louder.

"Well, it's one of the parables that Jesus told," Jordan began. His eyes widened as he stared at her left shoulder as the scratchy voice grew more frantic.

Kaylee took her right hand and made circles in front of herself to gesture her impatience for him to continue.

Jordan ignored her rudeness and focused his eyes back to her. "Basically, Jesus told the story of a poor man named Lazarus. He was covered in sores and sat at the gate of a rich man who ignored him and stepped over him everyday, never helping him. One day, they both died. Lazarus went up to Heaven, while the rich man went to hell where he was tortured for eternity. Even in death, the rich man thought Lazarus was not his equal. He begged Abraham to send Lazarus to bring him some water. Abraham said no and reminded him how he lived in luxury on earth and never helped ease the suffering of Lazarus. Lazarus suffered on earth but remained faithful, so he would now enjoy Heaven for eternity. The rich man enjoyed a good life on earth but chose to ignore God, so he would now suffer in hell without God's love or goodness for eternity. Then the rich man asked if Abraham would send Lazarus to warn his brothers to live better lives so they wouldn't end up in hell. Abraham said no, if the brothers wouldn't listen to the prophets, they wouldn't listen to a dead man."

The voice grew more frenzied, trying to convince her how cruelly the rich man was being treated. She could hardly think straight. "So what does it mean?"

"Well," Jordan said thoughtfully, "this is a broken world because humans chose to bring sin into God's perfect world. Because of that, bad things happen to even good people. We can't expect a perfect life if we are Christian. God doesn't promise that because this is a world full of sin. We aren't supposed to let that detract us from trusting and loving God. And if we do, He does promise to be at our side and love us. No matter how bad it gets here, we are supposed to keep our eye on the prize, which is Heaven. My dad says this life is but a blink of an eye, but eternity is forever. Kaylee, you need to protect your soul or you will spend an eternity in hell. We can catch glimpses of one of the Fallen on your left shoulder. He looks like a winged Gollum from *Lord of the Rings*. We're all so scared for you. Please." He looked at her tenderly. "Please call for Cotravin. Please come back to us. Only you can decide to save your soul. It's your decision. Please come back."

"Your grandma knew what would happen," Mandy said gently. "She was warning you with her last breath." She placed a hand on Kaylee's shoulder.

Kaylee quickly stood up and walked away from them. She tossed her uneaten lunch in the garbage and slid the metal tray onto the conveyer belt. She hurried to the assignment check-in, signed in, and pushed a cleaning cart down the hallway. She wanted some time alone, which was normally dangerous. She reached the bathroom and stared in the mirror. Thoughts whirled around in her head. She realized how lost and depressed she felt the last few weeks. Finally, she made a decision. She concentrated.

"Cotravin," she whispered. "I'm sorry. Please help me. Please?"

Cotravin instantly appeared in full size and in his white armor. Suddenly, she saw a repugnant demon on her left shoulder. A scream caught in her throat. The demon abruptly grew to full size and started to brawl with Cotravin with swords. Kaylee threw herself against the wall and covered her mouth as they fought. The battle was intense and brutal. Kaylee started to pray for Cotravin, confess her sins, and thanking God for His divine mercy. As she did, Cotravin started to win. She prayed even harder. Cotravin's golden sword pierced the demon's heart. The demon let out a high-pitched shriek and disappeared. Cotravin walked towards Kaylee, becoming more solid with every step. Kaylee fell into his arms, sobbing.

"I'm so sorry! Please forgive me," she begged.

Cotravin held her tightly, stroking her hair. "I'm so sorry for your pain. I tried to reach you, but I cannot if you turn me away. God loves you so much that He gives you free will. You must choose His love... and mine."

"I was so hurt, so sad."

"Blessed are the poor in spirit, for theirs is the kingdom of heaven. Blessed are they who mourn, for they will be comforted. Blessed are the meek, for they will inherit the earth. Blessed are they who hunger and thirst for righteousness, for they will be satisfied. Blessed are the merciful, for they will be shown mercy. Blessed are the clean of heart, for they will see God. Blessed are the peacemakers, for they will be called children of God. Blessed are they who are persecuted for the sake of righteousness, for theirs is the kingdom of heaven."

Kaylee smiled and nodded. "I couldn't hear you before. I just felt so angry."

"That is when you are the most vulnerable. They wait for those moments. It is their favorite trick. But this trial will make you stronger now."

"I can't believe that Grammie is gone."

Cotravin gently took her face into his hands. "She is not gone. Remember the pregnant woman?"

Kaylee nodded.

"When she was pregnant, the baby was happy inside her. The baby wanted to stay there forever because she didn't know about the next life waiting for her. Then she went through labor, and as you witnessed, that was not easy. But then she was born, and it was more than she could have imagined. She will have many wonderful experiences and know more love now. Her mother loved her when she was inside of her, but now they can have an even closer relationship. Your grandmother's death was like labor, and she is now reborn into an even more incredible life. She is very happy and feels more love than she could ever know in this sinful world. She is Home."

Kaylee felt a heavy burden disappear from her. "She's Home."

Cotravin smiled. "Yes. The Almighty does not like suffering for His children. But death is not a terrible thing in His eyes because you come Home to Him. It is a happy thing to be born."

Kaylee smiled, understanding. "She's Home… and happy and loved."

Cotravin nodded, smiling.

"And I will see her again."

"Yes," Cotravin hugged her close, "but not before your time. Only the Almighty knows when it is your time to go."

Kaylee felt so free, so peaceful. She breathed deeply. "You smell really good. Like Christmas… fresh cut evergreen and cinnamon." She felt his chest bounce as he laughed. She looked up at him. "Hey, I can feel you. This is the first time." She hugged him close again and breathed in his scent deeply. "I love you."

Cotravin closed his eyes, enjoying the moment. "And I will always love you, Beloved."

"What in the world is that?" A startled guard asked when he saw them.

Cotravin shimmered, and even though Kaylee could see him, to the guard, he had disappeared. Kaylee looked at the guard innocently, "What is what?"

The guard opened his mouth then closed it. "Get to work!" He finally managed to bellow.

Kaylee plopped down happily at the table at dinnertime. The others gave her a high-five when the guards weren't looking.

"I wish I could give you a welcome back hug," Jordan's eyes danced when he spoke.

"I..." Kaylee looked down at her noodles, ashamed. "I'm so sorry..."

"It's OK," Mandy reassured her. "We understand and are just happy you're back."

"We have never prayed so hard in our lives," Jordan added. "We were like warriors."

"Speaking of warrior," Kaylee began. She told them in detail about the battle in the bathroom and how Cotravin turned solid. They looked at him in wonder and admiration. He humbly listened until Kaylee finished telling the story.

"It is our job to protect you from the Fallen," he said. "But we can't if you choose to send us away. Beware of despair."

Jordan slipped Kaylee a small Bible under the table.

"How'd you get this?" Kaylee whispered as she surveyed the guards to be sure they didn't see her hide it under her baggy orange shirt. "Religion isn't allowed."

Jordan smirked. "I found a guy who now has visitation privileges and is a Christian. Can you believe he was sent here because he was passing out mini-Constitutions on Constitution Day at his college last year? Anyway, he was able to smuggle one in for each of us. I marked some passages that you might find helpful."

The shrill buzzer sounded, ending their dinner. They trudged off to the next lecture section. Kaylee now realized how foolish the talks were. She imagined that Hitler used the same logic to entrap a nation. God didn't control the actions of any human and go against their free will, so what gave a man the right to do it? Hitler and other rulers like him were such monsters. She glanced at her left shoulder to make sure there was nothing there.

"Don't worry, Beloved," Cotravin reassured her. "It will never get that close to you again if you choose me. I won't let him."

Kaylee spent the next several days sneaking moments to read the Bible while cleaning the bathrooms.

A girl who worked with her whispered, "What ya readin' there all the time? I been watchin' ya. You changed lately. Almost happy. What ya got goin' on?"

Cotravin nodded his head. Kaylee scanned the area to be sure they wouldn't be noticed. Over the next week, she shared the passages that Jordan had marked with the girl. She shared Psalm 16, 23, 31, 38, 46, Luke 7:36–50, Luke 14:15–24, Luke 15, Mark 4:1–9, Matthew 25:1–13, John 4:4–42, and, of course, John 3:16–18.

The girl leaned in closer as Kaylee finished reading John 8:1–11 aloud, "'Let the one among you who is without sin be the first to throw a stone at her.' And in response, they went away one by one, beginning with the elders. So He was left alone with the woman before Him. Then Jesus straightened up and said to her, 'Woman, where are they? Has no one condemned you?' She replied, 'No one, sir.' Then Jesus said, 'Neither do I condemn you. Go, from now on do not sin anymore.'" Kaylee looked at the girl sitting next to her who had tears of relief streaming down her cheeks.

"Wow," she whispered. "That's so cool." She had a look of hunger in her eyes as she looked ahead at the next verses.

A loud noise startled them. The girl quickly grabbed the Bible and hid it under her shirt.

"What you lazy things doin'?" A guard yelled. "Git back to work!"

"Yes, sir!" They exclaimed as they jumped to their feet.

"Mikha'el said it is time," Cotravin remarked to Kaylee.

"Time for what?"

"The four of you have sowed enough seeds here." He motioned to the other girl who was already beginning to clean the mirror. She hummed as the light on her right shoulder grew brighter. "This one and the others your friends have been witnessing to can continue to learn now and spread the Good News in this dark place. You four have a different mission." Cotravin spread his wings and wrapped Kaylee in them. They walked out into the hallway. No one looked at her. Her heart was pounding, expecting to get stopped at any moment. But they didn't seem to even see her. She walked in confusion. She saw Fredouglass, Darwallace, and Mulana all walking down different hallways towards her with their wings folded forward. She realized that her friends wrapped in the wings were invisible to other people just as the angels were. The guards appeared to be sleeping in this section of the building. Cotravin raised his right hand. The locks clicked, and the door gently swung open. The four teens with their angels' wings wrapped around them, calmly walked out of the prison, and the doors closed and locked behind them.

Darius tilted back his head as they all came together in a group hug outside of the prison fence, "And the Lord shall set you free!"

Chapter 8

"OK," Mandy breathed. "Let's go home."

Darwallace gently shook her head. "I'm sorry, Beloved. We can't go home."

"What?" Jordan exclaimed. "Why?"

"You are all fugitives now," Cotravin explained, glancing at Kaylee, knowing she just realized that she didn't have a home to return to.

Darius ran his fingers through his hair. "OK, then. Now what are we supposed to do?"

Jordan looked off into the distance, "We head south. To Texas, the last stand in this fight."

"Yes," Fredouglass agreed. "That is the plan."

"What plan?" Mandy asked.

"Mikha'el revealed last night that the reason Jordan's family was moved to Illinois was to meet you three," Fredouglass explained. "Then when the time was right, he was to guide you south to meet up with other patriots to fight."

"In the past, the South was the cause of cancer in America and had to be righted by the North," Darwallace explained.

"Slavery?" Kaylee asked.

The angels nodded.

"But now, the North is the cause of cancer in America with worshipping their own power and so-called knowledge. They think they are superior to the Almighty who blessed this nation, while the South has clung to the Word. So now the South will rise again and save this country."

"Aren't there Ku Klux Klan and white supremacy groups in the South?" Mandy asked.

"There are evil people everywhere," Mulana answered. "But most Southerners are good, honest people."

"So we are supposed to leave our families and friends behind and go south?"

"For now," Darwallace said. "Yer leaving will give yer father the strength to do what he needs to do for the plan."

"Which is what?"

"Fight."

Mandy laughed. "Fight? You don't know my father very well. He'll complain and throw stuff, but in the end he won't fight. That's my dad."

"You would be surprised what people do when their family is threatened."

"Hero. Poor Hero is probably dead since—" Kaylee's voice cracked. "Since no one is there to take care of him."

"My little sister has been taking care of him since we were taken," Darius gently rubbed Kaylee's arm.

"I'm OK," Kaylee smiled. "Really. I know Grammie is happier now."

"We should probably get going," Jordan hugged Kaylee and then glanced at the reeducation facility. "They are going to notice that we aren't at the evening brainwashing session."

The four angels became solid. They put their arms around the humans from behind.

"What are you doing?" Darius looked over his shoulder.

"Hold on tight," Mulana flexed and spread her wings.

"No way!" Darius shook his head. "I'm too heavy for you."

Mulana raised an eyebrow then lifted off, carrying Darius with her.

The others followed. The wind whipped Kaylee's hair as they flew just above the trees. Soon, they flew over cornfields that spread for miles in every direction. Cows in the pasture mooed as the teens waved to them from above. The teens laughed. The sun faded, and the air chilled as the hours passed. The angels gently landed in a line of trees that separated two fields.

"We will stop for the night," Mulana stretched her arms when she released Darius.

"We are weaker when we are solid."

"Why?" Darius asked, rubbing her shoulders.

"It is not our natural state," she smiled at him. "We are spiritual beings." She kissed him on the cheek to thank him for his concern and shimmered into her other state. "Our energy levels are much higher than yours, which is why you normally don't see us. The Almighty slows down our energy levels during this mission just so you can see us glimmering. The solid state is even more slow so it really drains us."

Jordan's stomach growled noisily. "I'm starving."

"Well, there's plenty of corn around," Kaylee pointed, leading the others into the field, the golden stalks waving over her head. "Let's go get some."

"Thou must not steal," Cotravin stated.

The teens stopped and looked at the angels.

"There's lots of corn," Kaylee complained. "They won't miss a few ears."

"The farmer did not give it to you."

"So what can we eat?" Darius asked.

"The Lord will provide," Mulana stated.

Instantly, a white flaky substance appeared on the grass, and water flowed from a huge rock.

"What is that?" Mandy asked.

"Dinner," Darwallace smiled.

"Dinner?" Darius picked up a piece and smelled it. "Can't He whip up a double bacon cheeseburger?"

Jordan walked over and picked it up, examining it. "Is this what I think it is?"

The angels smiled and nodded.

"What is it?" Kaylee inquired.

"Manna!" Jordan laughed and tasted a piece.

"What's manna?" Mandy asked, picking up a piece.

"It's what the Israelites had to eat in the desert after they left Egypt," Jordan took another bite. "Mmmmm, it's sweet."

70

The angels all nodded.

"Does it have a lot of calories?" Mandy asked.

Darwallace laughed, "No, Beloved. 'Tis very healthy for ya."

The teens started to eat the manna slowly, not sure about it at first. But soon they started filling their mouths with the sweet flakes until they were very full. Darius cupped his hands and drank from the rock. "Ahh, it's really fresh." He paused after he sat down. "Any chance this trick works for chocolate milkshakes?"

Kaylee shivered. Jordan held her close and rubbed her back. Mandy put her head on Darius's shoulder and closed her eyes, sighing contently, smirking when she heard his heartbeat speed up at her touch.

"I guess we should all get a little shut eye," Jordan said. They leaned against a tree and snuggled together to keep warm. The angels spread their wings tip to tip, surrounding them. Soon, the air was toasty and comfortable as if they were in the midst of a campfire. They drifted into the first peaceful sleep they had in weeks.

A noisy crow woke them up in the morning. They all groaned.

"Can't you guys shut him up?" Darius asked, stretching.

Fredouglass nodded slightly to the crow; it sat quietly on the branch. "We should go soon."

Manna appeared, and they ate their fill.

"Dunkin' Donuts should get the recipe." Jordan licked his fingers. "The Manna Muffin."

The angels turned solid, hugged them from behind, and lifted off. The flat landscape turned hilly. The scenery was gorgeous as they flew over the trees in the Smokey Mountains. The red, gold, and orange leaves danced across the landscape, giving a dazzling show. The sun transformed to orange and splashed across the sky, merging the earth and the heavens in a spectacular lover's embrace. The teens were overwhelmed with this glimpse of the Creator. The angels landed.

"Follow this path," Cotravin pointed to the dirt path as it wound up a hill through the woods.

"It will take ya to an inn," Darwallace shimmered out of being solid.

"When you meet the innkeeper, say 'God bless America,'" Mulana stretched as she shimmered.

"After his response, say 'Land of the free,'" Fredouglass instructed.

"That's weird," Mandy wrinkled her eyebrows.

"Is it code?" Darius asked. The angels nodded. "Yeah, it's like my brother used to tell me. He's in Afghanistan fighting right now. He's a Navy Seal, and they have special codes when they meet up with contacts."

The angels nodded.

"Cool," Darius started walking, "Let's go."

The teens walked up the path until it spilled into a clearing. There was a sprawling building with a wraparound porch. A large sign announced the Heaven's Gate Inn. The teens smiled at the guests who were rocking in the chairs, drinking coffee or tea, sitting in pairs under quilts throughout the sprawling porch, whispering secrets. They walked up to the check-in counter.

The man looked them over, suspiciously. "May I help you?"

"Yes, umm, we would like a couple of rooms please," Jordan sifted his weight uncomfortably.

"Sorry," the innkeeper crossed his arms. "Can't help you."

"You mean there's no room at this inn?" Jordan looked at Fredouglass. "Ironic. Are we supposed to sleep in the barn by a manger?"

"Y'all look a bit young to be needing rooms." The innkeeper eyed them judgmentally. "Why don't y'all go on home now."

"God bless America," Darius said quietly.

The man looked surprised. He cocked his head and said slowly, "and Lady Liberty."

"Ummm," Darius thought hard, trying to remember the next line. "Land of the free."

The innkeeper smiled broadly. "Home of the brave." He glanced around to be sure no one was around. "Wow, they are recruiting kinda young, ain't they?" He shook each one of their hands warmly.

Darius nodded. "We sort of got pulled in."

"Ain't we all?" The innkeeper laughed. "I thought y'all were just looking to hook up, as you kids say."

"No, sir, we're on a mission. Can we stay the night? Maybe get some dinner, please?" Jordan asked.

The innkeeper nodded. "Sure, sure. It's your lucky day. I have one suite open. It has two adjoining bedrooms. That will be $400."

The teens all exchanged glances.

The innkeeper sighed. "Y'all don't have money?"

"We sort of had to leave in a big hurry," Mandy chewed her lip.

"Tell him you will work," Cotravin said.

"We can work," Kaylee smiled sweetly.

The innkeeper nodded. "Well, I am a bit shorthanded, I guess. One girl just went home sick, and the other one is complaining about needing time off." He pondered the situation. "Alright, then, I'll tell Maggie she can go home. I already served dinner but still need to clean up the kitchen. Locals will start coming in for drinks and entertainment in less than an hour. Y'all can help with that. I guess you can clean the rooms too. Only a couple of nights now, I can't afford to be a charity even for the cause."

The teens all nodded.

"I'll show you to your room first," he gestured to them to follow. "No offense, but y'all are a bit ripe. You need to clean up before you serve." He looked at their empty hands. "Don't they give y'all any supplies when they send you out? I guess you should grab a clean set of clothes from the gift shop and some toiletries."

They followed him to the gift shop and picked out some clothes and personal items. They followed him up the stairs and into a suite. The girls shrieked in excitement at the beautiful room decorated in blue and gold with antique furniture dating to the 1800s.

"It's like being in *Gone with the Wind!*" Kaylee spun around in the middle of the room.

The innkeeper smiled. "Glad you like it. Hurry now, I need you downstairs in forty-five minutes." The innkeeper left.

"So," Darius smiled, running his hand through his hair. "How we going to divide up the rooms?"

The girls laughed as the angels all glared at him.

"I was just asking," Darius shrugged innocently.

The girls went into the other room and took turns showering after the boys did the same. Kaylee closed her eyes and let the warm water wash over her aching muscles. She squirted some of the shampoo into her hand and was delighted with the coconut smell. She lathered her hair twice to make sure it was clean, relishing the luxury after the reeducation center. The oversized towel was a soft hug as she wrapped it around her wet body. She actually enjoyed brushing her teeth, surrounded by the quaint tiles in the bathroom. It was wonderful to feel clean again. She put on some makeup she got from the gift shop, slipped on the clothes, dried her hair, and joined the others. They hurried downstairs. They gulped down some leftover ham and bread and washed it down with some sweet tea. The teens were surprised at how full the main room had gotten. All thirty small tables were full as well as the ten seats at the bar.

"Thanks for nothin'! What am I supposed to do?! It's Friday night!" The innkeeper slammed down his phone.

"What's wrong?" Mandy asked.

The innkeeper shook his head. "My singer up and left for Nashville with Maggie, leaving me high and dry. What am I going to do? I depend on nightly entertainment to bring in a crowd."

Fredouglass smiled and motioned to Jordan. Jordan shook his head. Fredouglass frowned. Kaylee noticed the exchange. Fredouglass caught her eye and nodded towards Jordan. She smirked. "Jordan, you can sing, right?"

Jordan glared at Fredouglass and then at Kaylee.

The innkeeper brightened. "Can you sing, boy?"

Jordan sighed. "I sing in church but..."

"Do you know any country?"

Jordan hesitated.

Darius put his arm around Jordan's shoulder. "He's from Texas. Of course he knows country!"

"Wonderful!" The innkeeper dragged Jordan to the stage and pointed to a guitar resting on a stand. "You're an answer to a prayer."

The crowd clapped politely as Jordan strapped on the guitar, shaking. The innkeeper stepped to the mike. "Thanks for coming out. You'll be glad you did because we have a real treat for y'all tonight."

Jordan shook his head slightly when the other teens grinned at him as they walked around taking drink orders. "Evening. My name is Jordan, and like any good country singer, I started singing in church. So if y'all don't mind, I'd like to start with my roots and dedicate this first song to my seven friends who are very special to me and sharing a very interesting journey." He started plucking the guitar, several people clapped when they recognized "Jesus Take the Wheel" by Carrie Underwood.

Kaylee paused and stared at Jordan, surprised at how good he sounded. He was noticeably nervous at first, but the audience quickly warmed to him. Encouraged, he relaxed and enjoyed himself, his smooth voice captivating the room. The crowd cheered when he finished his song, no one louder than the angels who did flips up in the high ceiling to show their pleasure. He smiled sheepishly, which made him even more charming. He began to play "Something 'bout a Truck" by Kip Moore followed by "Something to be Proud of" by Montgomery Gentry. The people obviously liked him with their enthusiastic applause and hoots and hollers.

The innkeeper scanned the room with a big smile on his face. The men were flirting with Mandy and Kaylee, ordering more drinks than usual so they would get a chance to wink at them. The women flirted with Darius as he served them and blushed when Jordan caught their eye and rewarded them with his dimples as he sang. "I changed my mind. You kids can stay as long as you want," he said to himself.

The audience's cheer was almost deafening when Jordan started singing "Friends in Low Places" by Garth Brooks. They raised their mugs of beer and sang along. Jordan sang for three hours with a few breaks. He sang a variety of songs by popular artists such as Blake Shelton, Dierks Bentley, Keith Urban, Luke Bryan, Kenny Rogers, John Denver, Neil Diamond, the Eagles, and Bon Jovi. The crowd clapped and rose to their feet when Jordan finished, waved, and took off his guitar. He trotted down the stage steps, grabbed Kaylee by the waist, and twirled her around.

"Whew!" He laughed with her and put her back down. "Now that was fun!"

"I thought you could only sing in church," Kaylee gushed, letting him pull her close. "You were fantastic." They kissed until Cotravin cleared his throat.

"Better hurry up with those dishes so everyone can get some sleep." Cotravin encouraged.

Kaylee glared at Cotravin, smiled sweetly at Jordan, glared at Cotravin again, and walked away. The teens cleared away the glasses and bottles and wiped off tables. Most of the male patrons slapped Jordan on the back, and the giggling women slipped him tip money as they left. Kaylee watched and rubbed the table furiously.

The teens gathered when all of the customers were gone. They piled their money on a table and started to count. The innkeeper came over and whistled. He collected it all.

"Almost paid off your debt," he smiled. "Of course, tomorrow is another $400."

"Isn't there a cheaper room?" Darius asked.

The innkeeper scratched his head. "Well, you could stay in the storage shed. It has some old beds in it. Ain't much, but I'll let you sleep there and give you food if you serve meals, clean the kitchen, clean the twelve guest rooms, and Jordan here sings. You can keep your tips."

"Deal!" All four teens held out their right hands for a handshake.

"Why don't y'all enjoy the suite tonight? This will pay for the gift shop stuff and discount on the room." The innkeeper walked away, counting the money.

The teens finished loading the enormous dishwasher, washing and drying the larger pots that wouldn't fit. They groaned and walked slowly up the stairs. They hugged each other goodnight and went to their rooms. The boys fell on their king-sized bed.

Darius perked up. "One of the girls is running a bath. Bet she's soaking in that fancy tub. Wonder which one?" He winked at Jordan as the angels folded their arms in objection. "Think they remembered to lock the door on this side?"

"I'm so tired," Jordan stretched. "I don't even care."

"Hey, man," Darius rolled on his side and propped up his head with his hand. "You were awesome tonight."

"Thanks," Jordan smirked.

"Never knew you could sing."

"You would if you went to church," Jordan cradled his head with both hands as he stared up to the ceiling.

"I go to church," Darius got up and dug through the gift store bag for his toothbrush. "I go to the Methodist Church."

"That's cool," Jordan motioned for the bag. Darius tossed it to him. "I been singing in church since I was little."

"You should be on *the Voice*," Darius suggested. "I caught Kaylee staring at you ever so dreamily." Darius fluttered his eyelashes.

"Yeah?"

"Yep," Darius laughed as he went into the smaller area outside the bathroom that contained a sink and mirror and put some toothpaste on his toothbrush. "Hey, isn't it funny how the girls were going on and on about the rooms?"

"Yeah," Jordan joined him and squeezed the toothpaste. "What is it with chicks and bed-and-breakfast inns?"

"They went on and on about how beautiful the canopy bed was. 'We're just like princesses.'" Darius mocked their voices.

"And they talked forever about the textured cornflower blue wallpaper. I never even heard of cornflower blue before."

"It is a pretty blue," Darius spit some toothpaste.

"Yeah," Jordan kept brushing.

"And the antique furniture with the 'fancy scrolled legs,'" Darius added.

"And the 'charming' Queen Anne chairs with the soft material."

They both spit, rinsed, and put their toothbrushes in the glass. Darius picked up the tiny soap in the fancy golden dish. "I bet they talked for an hour about how adorable this heart-shaped soap is."

"And how good it smelled," Jordan sniffed it. "Mmmm. Vanilla almond."

Darius sniffed it. "Mmmm."

The boys briefly listened at the adjoining door until the angels shooed them away. They turned out the light by the sink and walked to the king-sized bed.

"They went on and on about how 'lovely' this bedding is." Darius ran his hand over the covering. "With its cornflower blue swirls and gold trim on an 'exquisite' lace background."

Jordan ran his hand over the covering. "Yeah. You just sleep under it. Who cares if it's the prettiest bed thingy you ever saw?"

They got into the bed and turned out the nightstand lights. There was a long pause.

"How soft are these sheets?" Jordan asked in the darkness.

"They're incredible!" Darius answered. "It's like sleeping on soft bunny fur or a cloud."

There was another long pause.

"Want to toss around a football tomorrow if we can find one?" Jordan asked.

"Dude," Darius answered, "I think we need to."

*****

The next morning, the teens served breakfast to the couples that were staying at the inn. They changed the sheets on the beds, tidied up the rooms, and cleaned the bathrooms. None of the guests were around for lunch since they were all out on tours, so the teens moved into the storage shed. It was a wooden building with a couple of old bed frames and mattresses with lots of other clutter. They vacuumed off the beds and put on the worn bedding that the innkeeper gave them. Dust and cobwebs covered the window.

Mandy put her hands on her hips. "Not exactly like our suite from last night."

Kaylee sighed, "No. It was sure nice."

"We didn't even notice," Jordan commented. Fredouglass and Mulana covered their mouths and laughed.

Darius jumped on a bed, and it let out a loud creak. "How long we gonna be here?"

"Mikha'el said our target is coming tomorrow afternoon. He rented out the inn for just his people," Fredouglass said.

"Who?"

"Mr. Reid."

Darius sat up quickly. "I hate that guy!"

"You shouldn't hate," Mulana scolded.

"I seriously have a lack of love for that guy."

Mulana rolled her eyes, but everyone could see the slight smile in the corner of her mouth.

"What are we supposed to do?" Jordan asked the angels.

"He will be carrying information that we need to copy from his computer and get it to the patriots who can expose him," Fredouglass explained.

"How are we supposed to do that?" Kaylee asked, wiping off some dirt from the windowsill with a cleaning rag.

"You clean his room, download information onto a USB, and we will be told where to take it. But you have to be careful," Darwallace warned. "He has armed bodyguards."

"Oh, sure," Darius sighed. "Sounds easy."

"If they shoot at us," Jordan added, "we can hit them with our feather dusters."

"No," an angel they never saw before dropped down through the ceiling. "You have these." She became solid and gave them four guns.

"Who are you?" Mandy asked.

"I am working with the patriots even though they don't know it," she explained. "I have made you known to them, and they need your help."

"I don't know if I could kill anyone," Kaylee asked, looking at the gun.

"These are army grade tranquilizer guns," the angel explained. "Your Guardian Angels can protect you from most things, but angels are not allowed to hurt other humans. You have to do the fighting. Keep these on you at all times."

"Thank you." Jordan worked over the situation in his mind. "Why does a guy working at the Department of Education have armed bodyguards?"

"That is what you need to find out. Something just isn't right." The angel nodded, shimmered, and flew away.

"You better get ready for the dinner shift," Cotravin suggested.

After the last guest went out onto the porch when dinner was over, the teens quickly cleared the dishes. They went into the bigger entertainment room and started seating the evening crowd, a mixture of guests and locals. Some faces were familiar from the previous night, greeting them as if they were long lost friends. They gave song suggestions to Jordan, and he quickly wrote them down.

At 7:30 p.m., Jordan climbed the stage steps to fervent applause. He shyly smiled as he put on the guitar strap and sat on the stool. He started his set with "Summer of '69" by Bryan Adams. The crowd cheered. He went into "Real Good Man" by Tim McGraw.

"Mmm, I'll say," a woman said to her friend as Kaylee gave them a full peanut basket and took their empty glasses. "He *is* a real good-lookin' man!"

"Oh, stop!" Her friend laughed. "He looks like he's only eighteen, still wet behind the ears."

"So?" The woman giggled. "I like 'em fresh."

"Hey, honey," the friend looked at Kaylee, "would you mind sendin' that cutie for our drinks?" She motioned towards Darius.

Kaylee forced a smile and nodded. "Wonder if they'd care Jordan and Darius were only sixteen," she said under her breath, clenching her teeth.

Cotravin chuckled.

"This special request goes out to a couple celebrating their twenty-fifth anniversary!" Jordan looked at the piece of paper in his hand before dropping it. "Here's to Greg and Debbie!"

The crowd cheered and held up their drinks to the happy couple. Jordan picked out a pretty melody on the guitar and sang "I.O.U" by Lee Greenwood. The man stood up and held out his hand. The crowd sighed and clapped as the woman stood and slow danced with her husband. There wasn't much room, so the couple swayed in place as they held each other.

Darwallace noticed Mandy watching the couple longingly.

"That reminds me," Darwallace whispered to Darius. "You never got to take Mandy to that dance."

Darius nodded absentmindedly, leaning on the bar, closing his eyes to rest.

Darwallace glared at Fredouglass.

"Nice song to dance to," Fredouglass hinted.

Darius nodded, yawning.

Darwallace huffed, turned solid momentarily, punched Darius in the shoulder, and then quickly shimmered again. The innkeeper knitted his eyebrows, rubbed his eyes, and shook his head. He chuckled and dismissed the scene.

"Ouch!" Darius complained.

"Are you daft, man?" Darwallace inquired. "Ask the lovely lass for a dance!"

"OK, OK," Darius rubbed his shoulder. "But I don't think angels are supposed to hit people."

"I've always been an angel with some fire so to speak," Darwallace winked. "I think it's the red hair."

Darius rubbed his shoulder as he walked over to Mandy. He pulled Mandy into his arms and danced with her in place by the bar as they waited for the drink orders. "We never got to go to the dance. Let's not waste such a pretty song."

Mandy smiled and placed her cheek against his, swaying to the music, longing for the song to last all night. Kaylee watched them and sighed, wishing she could dance with Jordan. Everyone applauded when the song ended, and the couple took a bow before they sat down. The woman blew Jordan a kiss of thanks.

The crowd exploded when Jordan started singing Carrie Underwood's "Wasted." Jordan ended his night with Elvis Presley's "I Did it My Way." He collapsed in a chair when the last customer left. The teens piled their tips on the table and counted their money. They wiped off the tables and cleaned the kitchen. Kaylee held Jordan's hand as the four of them walked to the storage shed. They brushed their teeth in an old work sink with rusty faucets.

Kaylee hugged Jordan then gazed into his eyes. "You were amazing again tonight."

"Thanks. I think you're pretty amazing every night." He leaned in and gave her a long kiss.

Cotravin cleared his throat.

Kaylee wagged her finger at him. "So help me if you say 'chastity.' I'm…! I know, alright?!"

Kaylee stormed off and got under the quilt. Jordan took a slow breath and crawled into the other bed as Fredouglass gave him a supportive smile.

Darius kissed Mandy goodnight and watched as she got into the bed with Kaylee two feet away. He looked at Mulana and stuck out his lip, pouting.

"No," Mulana simply said.

"You're killing me." Darius threw up his hands and begrudgingly crawled into bed with Jordan.

"What," Jordan asked him, "no kiss for me?"

Darius farted loudly. "There you go."

The teens and angels all laughed heartily, distracting themselves from thinking of the dangers the next day would bring.

*****

The next day, the boys helped load luggage into the various cars after breakfast. The men all slipped them a few dollars for a tip. The girls rang up the ladies' final purchases of homemade jams and crafts in the gift shop.

The angels flew them to a sweet little country Baptist church where they actually ran into some patrons. The patrons introduced them to the minister before the service started like they were long lost cousins. When the minister heard that Jordan could sing, he invited him to sing "He Raised Me Up." Kaylee smiled and closed her eyes, letting his smooth voice surround her like a warm embrace. The congregation congratulated him on a touching song after the service, and then the angels flew them back to the inn.

They met on the porch after they cleaned the rooms for the next group of guests. Soon, a line of six limos drove into view, a black snake slithering towards them. Men in blue suits identical to the agents who arrested Mrs. Whitman got out of the cars. A couple of pretty women in their twenties got out of one car followed by Mr. Reid.

The boys jumped up and emptied the luggage onto a rolling cart, pushing it up the ramp on the side of the house to bring to the rooms. The girls ushered the people to the check-in and then showed them to their rooms, smiling sweetly to hide their disdain. The teens met in the dining room to set the tables for an early dinner.

"He's in our old room," Kaylee grunted. "Disgusting!"

They served dinner to the guests, twenty in all. The innkeeper cooked the meals himself and prided himself on the delicious cuisine. He came out and enjoyed the compliments from the guests. He encouraged them to catch the show in the next room at 7:30 p.m. as they rose from their tables.

There weren't too many locals since it was a Sunday night, so only half the tables were full. Jordan started with "Redneck Crazy" by Tyler Farr. Then he sang "Citizen Soldier" by 3 Doors Down followed by "Courtesy of the Red, White, and Blue" by Toby Keith and then "God Bless the USA" by Lee Greenwood. The teens smirked as the annoyance registered on Mr. Reid's face every time Jordan sang a patriotic song.

"Dude," Darius laughed when Jordan took a break, "you are really ticking him off."

Jordan grinned. A table of locals held up empty beer mugs, so Mandy went over to serve them. They shouted their support to Jordan for his song choices as he went back on stage after his break and strapped on his guitar. Mr. Reid stood up, gave Jordan a disapproving look, and left the room. The blond woman who was shared his limo looked after him, back to Jordan as he began to sing "I Drive Your Truck" by Lee Brice, and motioned for another drink.

*****

The girls served sweet tea and cookies the next day as the guests gathered in a conference room. They tried to get a look at the documents, but the people were very careful to block their laptop screens. They met the boys in the hall outside of the conference room.

"OK," Jordan whispered, "let's go."

They walked carefully but quickly up the stairs and used the maid keys to enter Mr. Reid's suite.

Kaylee froze. "How can I get in without the passcodes?"

Cotravin concentrated. "Type in 'Americaeducationdownfall'."

"How do you know?"

"We can hack into any electronic device," he smiled.

"Handy," Darius glanced nervously over his shoulder.

Kaylee sat down at the laptop and began clicking the keyboard. The others held their breath and fidgeted for a few minutes.

"How's it going?" Darius asked impatiently.

"I'm working on it," Kaylee snipped. "There's tons of files in here with weird names and firewalls."

"You're really good with computers," Jordan complimented.

"My dad worked for a computer security company," Kaylee inserted the USB and began copying files. "He taught me a few things before he took off."

The floorboards squeaked outside the room. Kaylee quickly lowered the laptop so it was almost closed. The four of them ducked into the closet as the door to the room opened. Mr. Reid walked over to the laptop and opened it, not noticing the USB. He knitted his eyebrows when he noticed he was already logged in but assumed he didn't log out from earlier. He took a deep breath, clicked on Skype, and immediately an elderly man appeared on the screen.

"I assume all is going according to plan," the elderly man twirled brandy in a crystal goblet.

"Yes, sir," Mr. Reid's voice was unusually shaky. "We have our trained teachers in place and the old ones out. The leader children are already violating the regulations to decrease competition in academics and athletics so they are being sent to our retraining facilities in droves. The remaining ones are just sheep. We also have the bill about to be passed that any student who does not meet in standard testing will also be sent to reeducation centers. This way we can get the students in parochial schools and the homeschoolers. New dormitories are being built all over the country to house them. Soon, all of the children will be under our control."

The elderly man sneered. "Good. Good. This was easier than I thought."

Mr. Reid smiled at the compliment. "Yes, sir. Most parents don't bother to check the material. They are too distracted with the bad economy. They have no idea. And they have no idea how to fight the legal system or have the finances to do it."

"Carry on." The elderly man disappeared from the screen.

Mr. Reid closed his eyes and sighed in relief. He shut the laptop and carried it out of the room with him.

"Now what?" Darius complained as they tumbled out of the closet. "He took the USB."

"You have to get it," Fredouglass instructed.

Kaylee and Mandy went to the kitchen and cut pecan, cherry, and apple pies. They put them on decorative dessert plates. Darius grabbed a slice of pecan pie and shoved a big bite into his mouth. Mandy put a hand on her hip.

"What?" Darius ate another big bite. "Spies can't get hungry for pie?"

The girls shook their heads, cut another piece, and placed the dessert plates on large silver trays. They carried them into the conference room. Kaylee went over to Mr. Reid. She smiled sweetly at him as she set a piece of cherry pie before him. He leaned over to whisper something to his colleague on the right. Kaylee carefully pulled the USB out of the port with her fingers as she picked up a dirty napkin. She nodded to Mandy, and they hustled out of the room.

The teens quickly plugged the USB in a complimentary guest computer in another room and scanned over the documents. The first page had a timeline starting with the 1970s. Under the date, it read "introduce textbooks that demonize America with Native American treatment and slavery." The next date was the 1980s, and it had "decrease teaching of Founding Fathers and other American heroes." Under the 1990s, it had "infiltrate colleges with radical professors." 2000s had "use unions to skyrocket education costs." And 2015 had written "replace teachers with our trained teachers to mold children and lower competition to raise compliance." 2015 plus had written "remove all children from homes to be raised by government, start with 'lawbreakers' and foster children." The other pages went into detailed plans, most of them illegal and unconstitutional.

"Turn it off," Cotravin warned. "Now! Now!"

"Just a minute," Darius kept reading. "Holy smokes! These guys can't be serious."

"We are deadly serious," a chilling voice made them catch their breaths.

They slowly turned to find Mr. Reid walking through the doorway towards them. They froze.

"I thought I recognized you," he went on. "I couldn't place it, but now I remember. You were in that rebel teacher's classroom in Illinois."

They stared at him, not knowing what to do.

"But what are you doing here?" He was more thinking out loud than asking them. His eyes fell on the computer screen, and he became furious. "What are you doing with that?! Who are you?"

Kaylee pulled out her tranquilizer gun and shot him in the chest. He clutched his chest, fumbled to pull out the dart, then collapsed to the ground.

Darius stood over him, nudging his unconscious body with his toe. "Nice shootin', Tex."

Jordan grabbed the USB and stuffed it in his jeans pocket. "I think it's time to check out."

The teens raced out of the inn and into the shed. They hastily grabbed their money and gift shop clothes when shots rang out and bullets splintered the wood. They all hit the floor.

"Any suggestions?" Darius asked out loud.

"Don't get shot," Fredouglass answered.

"Oh, you're just hilarious," Jordan ducked as more bullets tore through the shed. He went to a window, broke it with the back of his gun, and aimed at a blue suited man running towards them. Jordan shot, and the man clutched his leg then fell. "That's one for me."

Darius shot an agent. "And me." He shot again. "If only my mother could see me now... bet she'd take back all her complaining about me going paintballing before it was illegal."

Two men burst through the door. Jordan and Darius fought with them. Above them, the angels fought with demons. Kaylee and Mandy watched back and forth between the severe battles. Kaylee picked up a root beer bottle and smashed it on a blue suited man's head. He dropped. She aimed her gun and shot him to be sure he stayed down.

Jordan looked at her. "I have to admit this new side of you is so hot."

Mandy shot the man who was fighting with Darius.

"I had him," Darius complained as the man slowly dropped to the floor.

"I know you did," Mandy commented, rolling her eyes.

The teens ran out of the shed and into the woods. Several blue suited men chased them at a distance. Darius and Jordan quickly climbed trees while the girls ran ahead. They dropped onto a pair of men and fought with them. Jordan fell against a tree and shot both men with darts. Darius took the bullets out of the agents' guns and threw them as far as he could into the woods. They took off after the girls. Three more men in blue suits crept slowly towards them with their guns drawn.

Jordan popped out from behind a tree. "Yoo-hoo!"

The men all turned towards him. Darius let loose a heavy branch behind them that swung and knocked them out.

The teens stood over them and shot them in their legs with the tranquilizer.

"Now that was a cool trick," Jordan complimented.

"Thanks," Darius smiled. "My brother taught me some stuff."

"Enough fun for one day," Mulana turned solid with the other angels. "Time to go."

Kaylee shot another man in a blue suit as they rose above the trees.

"So hot," Jordan beamed at her.

Chapter 9

The angels landed them behind an armed man in fatigues. He turned, startled to see them, and scanned the sky as he aimed his gun at them.

"Hey, easy there, G.I. Joe," Jordan and the others held up their hands.

"God bless America," Mandy said.

The soldier snapped his attention on her. "And Lady Liberty."

"Land of the free."

"Home of the brave," he smiled and lowered the M16. He stepped forward and shook their hands. "Who are you, and how did you get this far into our headquarters?"

"You wouldn't believe us if we told you," Darius smirked at Mulana. "Now, can you take us to your leader?"

"Why?"

Jordan dug in his jeans and waved the USB. "A little data from the Department of Education."

The soldier leaned his head to his shoulder and talked into a walkie-talkie. "Falcon Patriot 5 Team 7 checking in. In possession of four patriots claiming intel. Over."

"Who are they? Over." Came a voice over the walkie-talkie.

"Tell him we're from Heaven's Gate Inn in Tennessee." Jordan flipped the USB and caught it.

The soldier repeated the information. There was a pause.

"Yes, we are expecting them. Surprised they got to Texas that fast. Send them in."

The soldier led them to a grassy hill. He grabbed a hidden handle and opened a door that led to a concrete ramp.

"Cool," Darius admired as he led them in.

The ramp emptied into a 150' by 150' room packed with small desks, people working on computers, and screens flashing with different news stations. There was a steady buzz of activity. A man in a uniform stepped over to them, shook their hands, and introduced himself as General Malcolm. He had graying hair and an aura of power and virtue.

"I believe you have some intel for us?"

"Yes, sir," Jordan handed over the USB.

"This is so cool," Darius admired the set up. "My brother would be all over this."

"Your brother?" The general inquired.

"Yes, sir," Darius smiled proudly. "He's a Navy Seal serving in Afghanistan."

"Ah," the general squared his shoulders in respect. "Good man. Unfortunately, our dear commander in chief has managed to drain our military by sending them out all over the world in bogus conflicts. She left our country almost completely defenseless."

"Defenseless against whom?" Mandy asked.

"Her." The general handed the USB to a soldier. "Get this analyzed immediately." He returned his attention to them. "The only troops left here at home in the official military are completely loyal to her and turning this country into a communist state. This little operation is unofficial and technically rebel."

The teens walked over and focused on the screens, soaking in the news stories from around the world. Suddenly, their parents, Mrs. Whitman, Darius's little sister holding Hero on a leash, and a crowd in front of Stacks appeared on a screen.

A reporter started to speak. "I'm standing here with the owner of Stacks restaurant who has defied the executive order by displaying Christmas lights and decorations." She turned to Mandy's father. "Why have you decided to do this? Isn't it pointless?"

Mandy's father looked into the camera. "I've been a law-abiding citizen all of my life. I lived simply, just running my restaurant and raising my family."

"Yes," the reporter sneered. "We did a background check and found that your daughter had to be removed from your home because she was involved in that destruction of property and horrific mall massacre in October."

"That's not right!" Mandy's father shouted. "The news reported it all wrong!"

A woman stepped forward, holding an infant. "This is Kaylee Amanda, and she wouldn't be alive if it weren't for them. I named her after the girls who helped bring her into this world under very difficult circumstances."

Kaylee and Mandy hugged, touched by the moving gesture of the woman naming the baby after them.

Mandy's father continued. "Mandy and her friends were innocent bystanders. They delivered this baby and disarmed the gunman. They are each kind, decent kids. We as their parents couldn't be prouder of them. They are heroes!" Mandy fondly touched her father's face on the screen, a tear running down her face.

The reporter was taken aback, at a loss for words because he was contradicting the narrative her news station had been running on the reckless teens. Mandy's father took her microphone.

"America, pay attention to what is going on," he pleaded into the camera. "Our government has forgotten its place. It runs our lives in every little detail. How can hanging Christmas lights up be dangerous? We have to remember our roots, who we are as a nation. I took it and took it and watched as this government crippled this country with debt and fear… and then they took my daughter away from me." His voice cracked. "She and her friends were imprisoned in that reeducation center, being brainwashed until they escaped. She can't come home because she will be imprisoned again. We are standing here as they take more and more of our children away. Well, no more!"

Mrs. Whitman took the microphone from Mandy's father and quoted from the Declaration of Independence. "When in the Course of human events, it becomes necessary for one people to dissolve the political bands which have connected them with another, and to assume among the powers of the earth, the separate and equal station to which the Laws of Nature and of Nature's God entitle them, a decent respect to the opinions of mankind requires that they should declare the causes which impel them to the separation. We hold these truths to be self-evident, that all men are created equal, that they are endowed by their Creator with certain unalienable Rights, that among these are Life, Liberty, and the pursuit of Happiness—that to secure these rights, Governments are instituted among Men, deriving their just powers from the consent of the governed—that whenever any Form of Government becomes destructive of these ends, it is the Right of the People to alter or to abolish it!"

The crowd cheered and Hero barked.

"America, it is time to stand up and fight this out of control government!" Mandy's father looked intently into the camera. "It's time to stand up and say YOU CANNOT HAVE OUR CHILDREN!"

The on location feed went dead, and the anchor sitting in the newsroom smiled into the camera. "Well, another whacko spreading crazy conspiracy theories," she nervously chuckled.

"Yes, Susan," her co-host laughed. "Is it any wonder why the government had to take his daughter away from him?"

Mandy removed her fingers from the screen. She slowly turned around to face the others, pride enveloped her. "That's my dad."

The general smiled. "People are finally waking up. We will leak your intel across the Internet. This will really help our cause."

"What cause exactly?" Kaylee asked as she hugged Mandy.

The general looked intently at each of them. "Saving the very soul of America."

*****

The teens spent the next three months training with the rebels. They learned to shoot, run missions, set traps, and sat in strategy sessions. They ran ten miles a day, climbed up ropes, trained in martial arts, and lifted weights.

Mandy admired her leaner body in the mirror after she set down the weights. "Hmm," she smiled. "Not bad."

Darius came up behind her, wrapping his arms around her, and kissed her neck. "I'll say."

Darwallace cleared her throat.

Darius rested his head on Mandy's shoulders, still holding her tight. "Is this chastity thing really necessary?"

All four angels glowered at him.

"Alright, alright." Darius reluctantly released her. "Shouldn't make her so pretty if I'm not supposed to touch her is all I'm saying."

"Centuries ago you would already be married so waiting was not a problem," Mulana smiled.

"So, not a problem?" Darius asked excitedly.

Darwallace drew her sword and pointed it on his heart. Darius immediately raised his hands. Darwallace drew closer to him, placing the sword point on his heart. "But yer culture changed when people get married now so don't be blaming the Almighty that your body is finding it hard to wait. Never forget, boy, that yer not married."

"I get your point." Darius cleared his throat. "Your very sharp point."

The teens showered and met in the intel room by the TV screens. News coverage talked about the spreading anarchy among citizens as they disobeyed the laws that impeded the Bill of Rights. In the South, children were put in hiding, and schools lay nearly empty as the information on the USB spread on the Internet like wildfire. In the rest of the country, parents started to question the government's authority in education. A grassroots organization started teaching about the Founding Fathers and the Constitution, led by Mrs. Whitman and the teens' parents. The sheep were beginning to fight the wolves.

The general came rushing in and signaled them to follow him into a smaller conference room.

"What's up?" Jordan asked.

"We just intercepted a drone strike order that President Effluent put out on David Sparton." The general spread out some maps on the table.

"Isn't he the guy who is the expert on American history?" Kaylee asked. "Mrs. Whitman uses his stuff all of the time. Why would they put out a hit on a history teacher?"

"He has an extensive collection of original writings of the Founding Fathers," the General explained. "They take out him and burn those writings—"

"They can rewrite our history," Jordan concluded.

"Exactly," the General concurred. "We have to get him and his collection here to safety. We can't get any communication to or from him. We believe he is being restrained and imprisoned on his own ranch. Several missions have failed. I don't know how you kids do it, but you seem to be able to get in and out of tight spots." He looked at each one of them. "Will you serve your country and accept this mission?"

The teens exchanged glances and looked at the angels who nodded. "Yes, sir."

The general nodded and began to explain the mission and showed them the maps. "You need to cover 252 miles from outside here in Dallas," he pointed on the map, "to Mr. Sparton's ranch outside of San Antonio before oh-four-hundred hours tomorrow morning. On foot." He looked at them questioningly.

"Sure," Darius answered, "No problem." The other teens nodded in agreement.

The general accepted their answer even though he didn't understand how they did it. "Get him, the documents, and hightail it back here before the drone strikes."

The teens went to the supply room and filled small backpacks. Darius picked up an M16 and waved it. Mulana shook her head and pointed to the tranquilizer guns. They held twenty darts each with a quick reload cartridge. They each stuffed several cartridges in their utility belts.

"Like Batman," Jordan joked, filling his utility belt.

"Yeah, man," Darius puffed out his chest. "But I'm Batman. You're Robin."

"Robin?" Jordan complained. "I'm not being Robin."

"Don't hate on Robin."

"Then you be Robin."

"OK, you be Batman, and I'll be Ghost Rider."

"Ooo, maybe I want to be Ghost Rider."

"That cool fire motorcycle.

"No, man. It's all about the fire horse."

The girls rolled their eyes and continued to fill the pouches on their belts.

"Fire horse?" Darius wrinkled his eyebrows.

"Yeah. The older Ghost Rider was from the wild west and had a cool fire horse."

"No, dude, the fire motorcycle is way cooler."

"But the fire horse can also be a friend."

"Hmm," Darius cocked his head to consider the argument.

Darwallace looked at Mulan and Fredouglass in disbelief. "Are you certain they are supposed to battle on our side in the war?"

Chapter 10

"How are those kids going to cover 252 miles, secure the writings, and get that guy off of that ranch undetected in less than eight hours?" An armed soldier asked his partner as they watched the teens sprint across the field.

"I don't know. But twenty bucks say they make it," his partner bet.

"OK," Cotravin called, "they can't see you anymore."

The angels became solid and scooped up the teens in midrun. They rose in the air and sped across the landscape. Darius turned his head and whispered in Mulana's ear.

"I told you to go before we left," she scolded.

They reached the edge of the ranch when the sun was setting. Jordan brought out the map and unfolded it as the others gathered around it. They each brought out night vision goggles and pointed out the surveillance cameras surrounding the ranch. The angels shimmered, wrapped around each of them, and they calmly walked past the two armed guards and the cameras. Darius put his thumbs in his ears, wiggled his fingers, and stuck his tongue out as they walked by the guards. Jordan laughed then quickly covered his mouth when the guards went on alert, looking around.

"Why can't we go out the same way?" Mandy asked.

"We will. David Sparton is a holy Jewish man, but his angel couldn't leave him to carry the books." Darwallace replied. "But now some of us can carry the books while the others guard all of you from the Fallen."

They walked through the foyer and noticed a light in another room. Darius motioned the others to follow, careful to avoid being seen by the cameras through the window. He peeked in the room and observed a senior reading in a stuffed leather chair. The walls were floor-to-ceiling bookshelves. A floorboard squeaked when the teens moved forward, and the anxious man looked up and then relaxed.

"Ahh," the older man slowly stood up. "My help has arrived. Elishun said you would be here tonight."

The teens walked into the room. They all bowed to the angel, Elishun, and shook the silver haired man's hand in greeting.

Jordan whistled as he looked around the room. "We have to carry all of these books?"

Mr. Sparton smiled. "My family has collected these for many generations. It is important to know history and learn from it. But you have to always look at the original."

"Primary sources," Mandy said.

"Yes, yes," the older man's eyes twinkled. "Very good."

Jordan pulled out a scrapbook that contained aged letters and writings. He carefully opened it and scanned it. He read the bottom signature. "Holy moly! This is an original letter written by Haym Solomon!"

"You know of him?" The older man was surprised.

"Yes," Kaylee walked over and looked at the letter. "He was a Jew who joined the Sons of Liberty and was arrested for being a spy. But after eighteen months, the British used him as an interpreter for their Hessian mercenaries. He helped some prisoners escape the redcoats and convinced the Hessians to not fight the Americans. He moved his family to Philadelphia after he escaped. He worked as a broker and helped work out the finances for the war. Matter of fact, in 1781, Congress and the head money guy, Robert Morris, told General Washington that they were broke when he asked for $20,000 for his campaign. General Washington looked them right in the eyes and said, 'Send for Haym Solomon.' Mr. Solomon raised the money and General Washington conducted the Yorktown campaign, which was the final battle of the Revolutionary War. And legend has it, he was also the guy who suggested the stars on the back of our money be put into the shape of the Star of David."

Mr. Sparton clapped enthusiastically and the other teens joined him. Kaylee jokingly bowed.

"Marvelous!" Mr. Sparton kept clapping. "You are a marvelous storyteller! I am so pleased that you young people are well-educated. Very unusual nowadays."

"Oh, we never learned that in school," Darius shook his head. "We only know that kind of stuff because of Mrs. Whitman, our teacher."

"You did not learn from this teacher in school?"

"No. She was fired for being too good."

Mr. Sparton nodded knowingly. "Very scary what is happening. The Department of Education asked me to help write the Common Core standards. The project sounded good at first. But the deeper I got into it, I realized that there was something wrong. When I objected to the corruption of the true American history, I too was fired."

"Mrs. Whitman uses your stuff all of the time."

"This is good to hear. I have made it my mission the past few years to save this country's history. But, come, come." He motioned to them to follow him. "While the angels do their noble work moving the writings, let us dine. I have prepared dinner."

Mulana and Elishun followed them. The other angels filled enormous canvas bags that the teens brought and made trip after trip carrying the books to the patriot headquarters over two hundred miles away.

"Mmmm," Mandy ate another bite. "Yummy potato pancakes."

"That's a big compliment," Darius took another piece of honey-glazed turkey. "Her family owns a pancake place."

"Then I humbly accept such high praise. I am glad to be able to serve you tonight for this is the last of my supplies," Mr. Sparton inclined his head. He leisurely gazed around the dining room table at his guests. "It is refreshing to have such wonderful companions. I have been trapped here for several weeks."

"How is that legal?" Jordan sipped some water.

"The NSA monitored my phone and e-mails. The government knew I was working with my good friend who runs a cable show to expose all of the lies they were teaching in so-called education. I had proof in my original documents." Mr. Sparton gently dabbed the corners of his mouth with his napkin. "Suddenly, I could make no calls or get on the Internet. Two men were posted outside and said they would shoot me if I left the house."

"That must have been terrifying." Kaylee put down her fork, her plate empty.

"My people are used to enduring trying times," he smiled. "I have a little trick to get through hard times without falling prey to doubt and depression. You need to avoid that because it makes you vulnerable to the Fallen."

Kaylee sighed knowingly.

"Would you like me to share it with you?"

The teens nodded eagerly and leaned forward.

"When I am going through hard times, I thank the Lord for His mercy for that exact circumstance. For instance, when my lovely Elsa died, I said to myself: what would I rather have? Have Elsa die and wait for me in Heaven or her still here suffering with cancer? I choose her to be happy and pain free in Heaven. Do I choose my body getting crippled but my mind sharp or a healthy body but weak mind? I choose a sharp mind. Do I choose the privilege of fighting for my sacred honor and country or live in fear and false peace? I choose to fight. So you see? I am getting exactly what I want, so I thank my God for His divine mercy that my life is exactly as it is."

"Wow," Kaylee tilted her head. "You make it sound so easy."

"Not easy, but simple. It is all in how you choose to look at life. God is greater than anything this life can throw at you. You will be much better in the fight if you approach it with a spirit of thanksgiving. Shed tears but always come back to giving thanks. The bad times teach you lessons and make you strong. Right now in this situation, I prayed. I could have panicked and fled, but I choose to believe. Elishun assured me that the Almighty had heard my cries and would send help. And here you are. I just could not leave the collection… all would be lost if it got destroyed." He looked around the table. "Now, tell me how you came to be my emancipators."

The teens told them of their adventures for the past few months. He listened intently, clicking his tongue in disapproval at their enemies' actions. The teens grew very fond of him in their short time together.

"Well, you are true patriots indeed." Mr. Sparton stood when their story concluded. "Shall we see the progress, my good friends?"

The teens followed him to the library. About twenty-five percent of the shelves were empty. Mr. Sparton nodded his head in approval. They settled in chairs and sofas in the family room. Jordan lit a fire in the fireplace at his host's request. They all listened with great interest as he told them story after story of the American Revolution and the Civil War. Soon, they all grew weary. A comfortable silence fell over the room as they watched the flames smolder in the fireplace. One by one, they drifted off to sleep.

"Danger!" Mulana shouted. "Arise! Fight!"

They woke from their sleep, hearts pounding. Mulana and Elishun battled six demons above them. The demons hissed and snarled as they attacked. The boys protectively wrapped their arms around the girls as they watched the spiritual war.

Four guards abruptly smashed against the door, splintering the frame. The teens leaped at them, using their newly obtained martial arts skills. Bodies fell over furniture, tables broke. The room was in chaos. Mr. Sparton huddled against the hearth and prayed as he watched the fierce fighting. The contest went back and forth; it was hard to determine who was winning. A soldier picked Kaylee up and threw her against the wall. His bleeding lips formed a cruel smile as he reached for his gun. On her back, Kaylee quickly drew her tranquilizer gun and shot him in the chest. He grabbed the dart in surprise and slowly collapsed to the floor. Since she was free from hand-to-hand combat, she could easily shoot the other three enemies. They hit the floor. The teens stood over the bodies, breathing heavily.

"Well," Darius sucked in air, wiping blood off of his cheek with the back of his hand. "That wasn't so bad."

Two more soldiers rushed through the broken door.

Jordan sighed, "Not done yet, I guess."

The boys engaged them in a fight. The girls tried to get a clear shot at each enemy, but the fight made them change positions so fast they were afraid of hitting the boys. They glanced up to the ceiling and saw that the angels were still engaged in their own melee.

"Anytime, ladies," Darius punched the soldier then executed a roundabout kick. The soldier grabbed Darius and forced him against the wall, his fierce face an inch from Darius's.

Mandy fired, and the soldier grabbed the dart lodged in his neck. The soldier widened his eyes in surprise as he slowly fell down.

"You almost hit me!" Darius bellowed.

"I'm sorry," Mandy was contrite and waved the gun. "It was really hard."

"Oh, standing there was really hard?"

"Well, I got him, didn't I?" Mandy's apologetic tone turned to annoyance. "Quit being such a baby."

Jordan landed a punch that knocked his opponent down. Kaylee shot the soldier and sarcastically blew into the nozzle of her gun like she saw in western movies. Jordan shakily saluted her as he tried to catch his breath. Machine gun fire exploded, and they dove to the ground as splinters and pieces of furniture showered on them.

The gunfire ceased. Dust from the debris filled the room.

"The Department of Education seems a bit overly aggressive," Darius whispered as he perked his head up from beneath his arms.

"Dealing with the Department of Defense must be a nightmare," Jordan uncovered his head.

"Are you OK, Mr. Sparton?" Mandy called.

They heard him cough from somewhere behind the overturned couch. "Yes, children," he coughed again. "Are you OK?"

"Just peachy," Jordan spit dust out of his mouth.

The machine gun fired another round into the room.

"OK," Jordan whispered when it was silent again. "This is getting old."

"Agreed," Darius shook his arm and debris fell off. "Let's go get them. You and Kaylee guard Mr. Sparton." As he crawled across the floor to the window, he glanced up at the other battle. "Great job, Mulana!" He yelled. "Show 'em who's boss!" He smiled when Mulana gave him a quick thumbs up before she picked up a demon and threw him across the room.

"She's feisty," Mandy complimented as they flipped out of the window into the shrubbery.

"That's why I don't smoke or listen to rap music anymore," Darius whispered, scanning the yard.

"There it is," Mandy pointed to a machine gun sitting in the back of a jeep. It was positioned next to a small barn. "Well, Batman. Let's put your utility belt to work and use that nifty rope thingy."

"I'm Ghostrider." Darius winked. "Jordan is Batman."

The teens crept behind various bushes and yard objects until they reached the backside of the shed. Mandy took out a gun and shot a hook onto the roof. She pulled the thin rope and nodded when she assessed it was secure.

"I just realized something," Darius pulled Mandy into an embrace. "We are alone. Mulana is busy with the demons, and Darwallace is two hundred miles away." He pulled her close and kissed her deeply.

Mandy smiled. "Tempting, but we are kinda on the clock." She winked and started to climb.

Darius and Mandy climbed the rope and crawled on the roof. They inched towards the edge and peered over. A lone soldier took a drag on his cigarette and fired another round into the house.

When he finished, he spoke into the walkie-talkie. "What's your ETA? They took out six of my guys. I'm alone here. Over."

"We should get there in ten minutes. Hang tight. Make sure they do not leave the house. That is imperative. Over."

"Roger that. I have enough ammo to keep them pissing in their pants."

Mandy and Darius exchanged smirks. Mandy held up three fingers and lowered them one by one. On three, they both jumped and landed on the soldier. The three of them tumbled to the ground and quickly sprawled to their feet. Darius landed a right hook, and Mandy shot the enemy with a dart as he staggered. The soldier folded to the ground.

Darius walked over and twisted the cigarette into the ground with his boot. "Smoking is hazardous to your health, dude."

"Let's dump him into the shed so they don't think anything is wrong if they come before we can get out of here."

Darius grabbed the soldier's feet as Mandy grabbed his arms. They started to carry him through the open shed door. Darius dropped the soldier and started hitting his shoulders and twisting around hysterically.

"Ahh, ahh!" He shouted as he turned. "I just backed into a big spider web!" He swatted frantically. "Is it on me?! Is it on me?!"

Mandy dropped the soldier's arms and clutched her stomach as she doubled over laughing.

Darius stopped turning and kept trying to look on his back. "It's not funny! Those things are creepy!" He shuddered.

They picked up the soldier, carried him into the shed, and latched the door. They started walking back to the house.

"Wow," Mandy commented as she gazed into the night sky. "Look at that moon and stars. Can't beat Texas."

"Yeah," Darius looked up. "You just don't get night skies like this in the Chicago 'burbs. And you are even more gorgeous in this moonlight." He kissed her deeply then slowly pulled back. "Oh, man, I can't believe it."

Mandy whispered, "What?"

"Now that we could fool around a bit because the angels aren't around," Darius rubbed his head, "I still know it's wrong. And, I guess I don't want to." He sighed. "I don't recognize myself."

Mandy hugged him. "I do. I think you are just a better version of yourself." She tenderly touched his cheek. "And I love this version."

Darius smiled and gently ran his fingers through her hair. "And I love your better version."

As they walked into the house, Mulana and Elishun thrusted with their swords of truth, and the demons let out a high-pitched shriek and disappeared.

"Lucy," Darius called. "I'm home."

"Whew," Jordan kicked a chunk of wallboard with his toe. "This place is a mess."

The other angels arrived, shocked at the condition of the room as well as the teens' faces.

Darius held up his hands as Mulana fussed over the cuts on his face. He glanced at Darwallace's shocked expression as she looked around the destroyed room. "I told Mandy we didn't have time for a party, but you know how she is."

"How long do those dart things last?" Kaylee looked around, worry on her face.

"It doesn't matter," Cotravin turned solid. "We finished and should go now. It is 3:58 a.m."

Mr. Sparton sniffed. "The government has no right to do this to a man's home." He wiped away a tear. "No right."

Mandy and Kaylee hugged him from both sides and patted his back as they all walked out to his yard. The angels turned solid, lifted them above the roof, and flew away hastily. When they were only thirty-three feet from the house, a drone whistled past them, and the house exploded, scattering decades of cherished possessions. Mr. Sparton covered his face with his hands and wept, then he chanted prayers of thanksgiving for God's mercy and their safety.

Chapter 11

"Medic!" the general bellowed as the weary teens and Mr. Sparton shuffled into the intel room.

A soldier handed another soldier a twenty dollar bill.

"Good God," the general shooed some workers out of their chairs so the group could sit down. "You really earned your stripes today."

"You should see the other guy." Jordan winced when a medic started to clean a cut on his cheek.

Darius eased himself into a chair. "I could really go for a soak in that fancy tub at Heaven's Gate Inn."

"Where did you put the documents?"

"Umm…" Jordan looked at the angels. Fredouglass nodded his head towards a hallway. "Right this way, sir." The medic frowned as Jordan stood before she had barely aided him.

The teens led him down the hallway while the medic attended Mr. Sparton. Cotravin stopped in front of a door and pointed. Kaylee opened the door. The general gasped as he stepped into the room to find it almost filled with stacks of books from floor to ceiling.

"How did you get these in here without us…? And cover that distance…? And…" The general stared at them in amazement. "How in Hades did you accomplish this mission?"

Jordan grinned. "Actually it's more like how in Heaven did we accomplish it, sir."

The general slapped them each on the back, not noticing them wince. "Well, if you liked that little party, I have another one involving you breaking into the NSA. Some nasty business going on there that the American people need to know about. You up for it?"

The teens exchanged looks between themselves and the angels. "Yes, sir!"

The general rubbed his hands together. "Excellent. Excellent. You kids are a big surprise, a secret weapon. You are true patriots and saving this country of ours. Now... you need an official codename for your team."

Kaylee thought. "How about Halo-Wing Patriots Team Eight?"

"Eight? But you only have four on your team."

The teens and angels laughed and placed their right hands on top of each other in the middle of their group and then raised them high over their heads.

The end... until the next battle

Notes

Please research topics that interest you.

Chapter 1
1. Guardian angels have been documented.
2. Cotravin combination of my sons' names: Cody, Travis, Austin.
3. Pets in Detroit were abandoned when the city fell.
4. Fredouglass refers to Frederick Douglass, an American hero.
5. Archangel Michael is the angel of courage and is Mikha'el in Hebrew.
6. American Covenant: Refer to *the Covenant: One Nation Under God* by Timothy Ballard.

Chapter 2
1. Americans gave up freedoms through accepting the Patriot Act after the 9/11 tragedy.
2. Several parents were arrested in school board meetings when they spoke against Common Core. Parents in Texas and Indiana rejected it in their states' education.
3. The Constitution protects us against an overbearing federal government... know your rights in order to protect them.
4. Most original documents, such as the Constitution and the Federalist Papers, are written in cursive writing. Common Core dropped cursive writing.
5. More people are on government food stamps and other programs than ever before.

Chapter 3
1. St. Thomas Aquinas stated that he did not believe that guardian angels could read our minds.
2. NSA (National Security Administration) is spying on all Americans' electronic communications according to leaks by Edward Snowden. Senator Rand Paul and FreedomWorks are suing the federal government to test the constitutionality of this practice.
3. Christians celebrate the sacrifice of Jesus Christ for their sins by following the Last Supper recorded in Matthew 26:26, Mark 14:22, and Luke 22:14. Roman Catholics and Lutheran Missouri Senate believe in the actual presence of Jesus in the Host and Precious Blood.
4. Lucifer, also referred to as Satan or the devil, grew jealous of God and was thrown out of heaven and into hell. Angels that chose to follow him are demons, also referred to as Fallen.

Chapter 4
1. Mrs. Whitman refers to Walt Whitman, a preacher and teacher who was important in educating the colonists in the Revolutionary War.
2. The Fourth Amendment protects citizens against search and seizures without proper warrants.
3. The president takes an oath promising to uphold the Constitution.
4. Mr. Bennedict refers to Bennedict Arnold, a traitor in the Revolutionary War.
5. Martin Luther King Jr. quote: "The ultimate measure of a man is not where he stands in moments of comfort and convenience, but where he stands at times of challenge and controversy."

Chapter 5

1. Mulana refers to Mulan, a heroine in China.
2. Primary sources that show that George Washington was a very devout Christian who ran church services for his troops and asked them to fast and pray before battles. There are also primary sources about how Washington was not hurt in a battle even though he had bullet holes in his coat and hat.
3. Darwallace refers to William Wallace, a Scottish hero who fought for freedom.
4. There were several attacks on shopping malls from 2010–2014.
5. Public Security and Reeducation Act is fictitious.

Chapter 6

1. Kaylee Jefferson refers to Thomas Jefferson, Founding Father and president.
2. Jordan Coolidge refers to Calvin Coolidge, president.
3. Mandy Lincoln refers to Abraham Lincoln, president who fought a civil war.
4. Marcus King refers to Martin Luther King Jr., preacher and civil rights activist.
5. When arrested, the person has a right to know the charge and be read the Miranda Rights.
6. Baily Gates refers to Bill Gates and entrepreneur spirit.
7. See Bible stories: Moses and Pharaoh (Exodus 2–13), David and Goliath (1 Samuel 17:32–37), Joseph (Genesis 37–45)
8. George Bambino refers to George Ruth (the Great Bambino) and sport excellence.
9. There was a seventh grade boy who was suspended from school for using a toy gun in his own yard on September 24, 2013.
10. Parable of Lazarus and the Rich Man in Luke 16:19–31
11. Affordable Care Act (Obamacare) has a provision for "death panels" where unelected bureaucrats will make decisions on care to control costs.

Chapter 7
1. Guardian angel doctrine states that they can only help if they are given permission.
2. The Beatitudes in Matthew 5:2–12 and Luke 6:20–26
3. Christians believe that believers go to Heaven when they die and never disappear from existence.

Chapter 8
1. Abraham Lincoln and the North led the fight in freeing the slaves.
2. The southern states have a higher population of Christians than the northern states.
3. Ku Klux Klan and white supremacy groups are racist and violent.
4. Manna is food given to the Israelites from God when they were in the desert (Exodus 16:31, Joshua 5:12, John 6:49, and Revelations 2:17).
5. Greg and I celebrated our twenty-fifth wedding anniversary on August 20, 2013 and celebrated in a bed-and-breakfast in the Smokey Mountains. It was wonderful!

Chapter 9
1. General Malcolm refers to Malcolm X.
2. Quote from the Declaration of Independence: "When in the Course of human events, it becomes necessary for one people to dissolve the political bands which have connected them with another, and to assume among the powers of the earth, the separate and equal station to which the Laws of Nature and of Nature's God entitle them, a decent respect to the opinions of mankind requires that they should declare the causes which impel them to the separation. We hold these truths to be self-evident, that all men are created equal, that they are endowed by their Creator with certain unalienable Rights, that among these are Life, Liberty and the pursuit of Happiness—that to secure these rights, Governments are instituted among Men, deriving their

just powers from the consent of the governed—that whenever any Form of Government becomes destructive of these
ends, it is the Right of the People to alter or to abolish it!"

3. The President of the United States has the power to order
a drone strike. Senator Rand Paul led a filibuster March
7, 2013 to get an answer on record as to the president's
power to order the death of an American citizen without
due process.

Chapter 10

1. David Sparton refers to David Barton who is a leading
American history scholar, collector of original artifacts and
documents, and founder of Wallbuilders.com. He is actually younger and a Christian.

2. The events of Haym Soloman are factual.

About the Author

Debbie Beeber is a proud mother of three sons and wife of a deacon/ engineer. She was born in Canada and moved to Illinois when she was five. She dreamed of being a writer and wrote stories in her free time but majored in education at Concordia College, River Forest and became a middle school science teacher. She happily taught middle school for many years; however, she had to recently retire due to health issues. Although it was difficult to give up teaching in a classroom at first, she used this opportunity to follow her dream and write this book to teach. She has a passion to help in causes such as the Nazarene Fund and plans to use profits from the sale of this book to donate to rescue children in the slave trafficking. She hopes this inspires people to find their divine purpose and follow their dreams.

CPSIA information can be obtained
at www.ICGtesting.com
Printed in the USA
FSHW011940101218
54386FS